THE GREAT GATSBY

GOLD EDITION

F. SCOTT FITZGERALD

EDITED BY
ADAPTIVE READER

ISBN: 979-8-8693-0815-3

CONTENTS

INTRODUCTION

Welcome to Adaptive Reader, your portal to the captivating world of literature, tailored to fit your unique reading abilities.

In today's fast-paced and diverse learning environment, we believe in the power of personalized learning experiences. That's where the concept of leveled reading comes in, and why we, at Adaptive Reader, have dedicated ourselves to offering a broad collection of classic novels at various reading levels. Our mission is to make the joy and benefits of reading accessible to everyone.

THE BENEFITS OF LEVELED TEXTS

So, what exactly is leveled reading? It's an approach that matches students with texts that align with their unique reading abilities. This ensures that every reader is challenged just the right amount - enough to grow, but not so much that they feel overwhelmed or frustrated.

For students, this means you'll engage with texts that stretch your reading skills while keeping the experience enjoyable and manageable. You'll gain confidence as you successfully comprehend each level and feel motivated to explore more challenging texts as your reading skills grow.

For teachers, Adaptive Reader provides a valuable tool to support differentiated instruction. You can assign the same novel to your entire class while ensuring each student reads a version that aligns with their reading level. This allows all students to participate in class discussions and activities, fostering a more inclusive learning environment.

For parents, Adaptive Reader offers a supportive tool to encourage your children's reading journey. As your child progresses through the different levels of a novel, they'll not only enhance their reading skills but also develop a deeper love for literature.

READING ACROSS MULTIPLE EDITIONS

All of our leveled novels include passage markers that correspond to the same content across every one of our editions. This means that passage '62' in our silver edition contains the same themes and plot elements as passage '62' in our original edition.

For teachers, this means that you can say "let's look at passage 35 together. What is the author trying to tell us here?" and all of your students will be reading the same content — but with vocabulary and syntax that's adapted to their reading level.

Our online reading tool, available at www.adaptivereader.com, gives students and teachers free access to the original text with passage markers. We encourage teachers to include close readings of the original text as part of their coursework, giving all students exposure to the rich original syntax and language of these exceptional authors.

THE POWER OF LITERATURE

At Adaptive Reader, we are committed to helping everyone experience the power of literature. So whether you're a student diving into a classic novel, a teacher looking for flexible resources, or a parent seeking ways to support your child's literacy, Adaptive Reader is here for you.

We invite you to embark on this exciting literary journey with us. Enjoy the world of stories, characters, and ideas that await you in our collection of leveled novels. Happy reading!

CHAPTER

ONE

DURING MY TEENAGE YEARS, my father shared some valuable advice that has stayed with me.

"Whenever you have the thought to criticize someone," he cautioned, "take a moment to consider that not everyone in this world is as fortunate as you."

He didn't say any more, but we've always been able to understand each other in a quiet way. I knew he meant much more than that. As a result, I tend to hold back from making judgments. This practice has allowed me to know many interesting personalities. However, this trait also caused me to become stuck talking to people I didn't want to. Because of this, people in college wrongly accused me of being social because I was nosy. People would they'd tell me things I didn't want to know, so sometimes I'd be rude on purpose or pretend to sleep, hoping they'd stop. Holding back judgment is an act of optimism. It might sound snobby, but as my father suggested, not everyone has the privilege of understanding and doing things according to the standard.

And, even though I claimed to be open-minded, I have to admit that there are limits to what I put up with. People may have different

1

reasons for their behavior. When I returned from the East last fall, I realized that I wanted more organization and politeness. I no longer wanted to indulge in wild adventures. The only exception to this was Gatsby, the man who is the focus of this book.

I had a genuine dislike for everything Gatsby represented. However, there was something captivating about Gatsby. He had a heightened sensitivity to the potential of life. It was like he was connected to a machine that could detect earthquakes thousands of miles away. He was creative and had the extraordinary ability to find hope in any situation. He had a romantic readiness that I have never seen in anyone else. What troubled Gatsby and the dark consequences of his dreams made me think differently about the sadness and happiness of others around me.

My family has been well-known and successful in a Midwestern city for three generations. The Carraways are a kind of extended family, and we have a belief that we are descended from the Dukes of Buccleuch. The true founder of our family was my grandfather's brother. He came here in 1851 and found someone else to serve in the Civil War in his place. He started the wholesale hardware business which my father now continues.

I never met this great-uncle, but I'm told that I look like him. I graduated from Yale University in 1915, twenty-five years after my father, and later took part in the Great War. I enjoyed the excitement of the war so much that when I returned, I felt restless. Instead of feeling like the vibrant center of the world, so I decided to move to the East and learn about the business of buying and selling bonds. It seemed like everyone I knew was involved in that field, so I thought there was room for one more single man. My aunts and uncles discussed my plans. My father agreed to support me financially for a year, and after various delays, I moved to the East for good in the spring of 1922.

The practical thing to do was to find a place to live in the city. With the help of a friend, I found a bungalow for eighty dollars a month. I had a dog, but he ran away after a few days, and a house-keeper from Finland.

For a day or so, it was quite lonely, until one morning when a man who had recently arrived in the area stopped me on the road.

"I'm lost," he said helplessly. "Can you tell me how to get to West Egg village?"

I gave him the directions, and as I continued walking, I no longer felt lonely. I felt like a guide, a pioneer, an original settler. I felt part of the community.

The sunshine arrived, as did leave on the trees. I had that familiar feeling that life was starting fresh again with the arrival of summer.

There was so much to read, first of all, and so much good health to be gained from the fresh air. I bought a dozen books about banking, credit, and investing, and they sat on my shelf with their vibrant red and gold covers. I also had a strong desire to read many other books. In college, I liked writing and wrote for the school newspaper. I wanted to be a "well-rounded individual." This isn't just a clever saying—life is often best understood through a single perspective, after all.

By chance, I ended up renting a house in an odd little place. This community is located on an island to the east of New York, and it's known for its unique geographical features. Specifically, there are two distinct land formations that stand out. Just twenty miles away from the city, two rocks that look like giant eggs can be seen jutting out into the tranquil body of water known as Long Island Sound, which is very peaceful. These eggs aren't perfect ovals. Instead, they're flattened on one side, resembling the eggs from the Columbus story. The seagulls flying above must find this physical resemblance fascinating. However, what's more intriguing to us, who don't have wings, is how these eggs differ from each other in every aspect except their shape and size.

I resided in West Egg, which was considered the less trendy of the two areas. However, this isn't the only way that the Eggs were different. My house was located right at the edge of the egg, a mere fifty yards away from the Sound, and it was squeezed between two enormous properties that were rented for twelve or fifteen thousand dollars per season. The one on my right was an enormous mansion that could impress anyone. It was a like a duplicate of a Hôtel de Ville in Normandy, complete with a tower on one side. It looked brand new, with only a thin layer of ivy. It had a grand marble swimming pool and over forty acres of perfectly manicured lawns and gardens. This extravagant estate belonged to a man named Gatsby. Well, I should clarify that I wasn't acquainted with Mr. Gatsby himself, but rather, it was a mansion occupied by someone bearing that name. On the other hand, my own house wasn't much to look at. Still, I had a view of the water and a glimpse of my neighbor's lawn. Plus, I had the soothing presence of millionaires nearby, all for the modest price of eighty dollars per month.

Across the bay, the fancy white palaces of fashionable East Egg sparkled along the waterfront. The tale of that summer truly begins on the evening I drove there for dinner with the Buchanans. Daisy, who happened to be my second cousin once removed, and Tom, whom I had known during our college days, were the hosts. After the war, I had spent a couple of days with them in Chicago.

Her husband, who was exceptionally skilled in sports, had once been one of the best football players at New Haven. He was widely known and admired on a national level, having achieved such great success at the young age of twenty-one that everything he did after-wards seemed like a disappointment. His family was extremely wealthy, and even during his college years, he was infamous for spending his money recklessly. Now that he had left Chicago and moved to the East, his extravagant lifestyle was even more evident. For example, he had brought a whole set of polo ponies from Lake Forest. It was hard to imagine that someone from my own genera-tion could be so rich.

I wasn't sure why they had chosen to move to the East. They had spent a year in France, going wherever wealthy people gathered to play polo. According to Daisy, their move to the East was permanent, but I doubted it. I had a feeling that Tom would continue to drift, always searching for the excitement and intensity he had once experienced on the football field.

That's why on a warm and windy evening, I drove to East Egg to visit two old friends whom I barely knew. Their house was even more extravagant than I expected, a cheerful red-and-white Georgian Colonial mansion that overlooked the bay. The lawn stretched from the beach to the front door for a quarter of a mile, passing by sundials, brick walks, and beautiful gardens. As it reached the house, the lawn extended up the side of the mansion, covered in vibrant vines that seemed to continue growing. There were grand windows, too. On the front porch, Tom Buchanan stood with his legs apart, wearing riding clothes.

Tom had changed a lot since his time at New Haven. Now, he was a strong straw-haired man in his thirties and very uppity. He had sparkling eyes and an aggressive posture. You could see a mass of muscles shifting as his shoulder moved beneath his thin coat. It was a body capable of great strength—an intimidating body.

His speaking voice was rough and he almost always seemed annoyed. Even towards people he liked. He had a hint of superiority in his tone. In fact, there were men at New Haven who didn't like him at all.

He seemed to be saying, "Now, don't think that my opinions on these matters are better just because I'm stronger and more masculine than you." In college, although we were never close, I always had the feeling that he approved of me and wanted me to like him.

We chatted for a few minutes on the sunny porch.

"I have a beautiful home here," he said, his eyes constantly scanning his surroundings.

Taking me by the arm, he turned me around. There was a sunken Italian garden, a spacious area filled with strong-smelling roses, and a small motorboat that bobbed in the tide offshore.

"It used to belong to Demaine, the oil tycoon." He turned me around again, politely but abruptly. "Let's go inside."

We walked through a long hallway into a brightly lit room filled with shades of pink. It was connected to the rest of the house by windows on both ends. The windows were slightly open, which made it seem like the fresh grass outside was creeping into the house. A gentle breeze moved through the room, causing the curtains to billow in and out like pale flags. They looked like waves on the sea.

The only thing that remained still in the room was a large couch on which two young women were seated. Both women were dressed in white, and their dresses fluttered and flowed. They looked like angels. Suddenly, there was a loud sound as Tom Buchanan closed the windows behind us. The curtains, rugs, and the two young women slowly sunk back to the floor.

The younger of the two girls was unfamiliar to me. She laid stretched out on one end of the couch, completely still. Her chin was slightly raised, as if she was trying to balance something delicate on it. If she noticed me entering the room, she gave no sign. I was so taken aback by her unresponsiveness that I nearly apologized for bothering her.

The other girl, Daisy, made an effort to sit up. She leaned forward with a serious expression, but then burst into a delightful, silly laugh. I couldn't help but laugh along with her as I approached.

"I'm so incredibly happy," she said, her voice filled with mirth.

She laughed again, as if she had made a clever remark, and held my hand while gazing up at me. She mentioned in a soft whisper that the balancing girl's last name was Baker. (I had heard rumors that Daisy whispered things in order to make people lean closer to her, but even if it was true, it only added to her charm.)

In any case, Miss Baker's gave me a barely noticeable nod before quickly straightening her head again. It seemed that whatever she was trying to balance had almost tipped over. Once again, an apology formed on the tip of my tongue. I always find myself in awe of those who show complete self-confidence.

I glanced back at my cousin, who began to ask me questions in a soft, captivating voice. It was the type of voice that you can't help but listen to. Her voice was like a song. Her face held a mix of sadness and beauty, with bright features like her eyes and passionate mouth. But it was the excitement in her voice that lingered in the minds of the men who had cared for her. She was hard to forget. Her voice made you want to listen.

I shared the story of how I had made a brief stop in Chicago on my way to the East, and how a number of people had sent their well wishes through me.

"Do they miss me?" she exclaimed ecstatically.

"The entire town is filled with sorrow. Every car has painted its left rear wheel black as a symbol of mourning, and there is a constant crying that echoes through the night."

"How marvelous! Let's go back, Tom. Tomorrow!" Then, as if it were unrelated, she added: "You should see the baby."

"I would love to."

"She's asleep. She's three years old. Have you never met her?"

"Never."

"Well, you must see her. She's—"

Tom Buchanan, who had been pacing the room and interrupted.

"What are you up to, Nick?"

"I work in the bond business."

"With whom?"

I told him.

"I've never heard of them," he stated firmly.

That comment irritated me.

"You will," I replied quickly. "You will if you stay in the East."

"Oh, I'll stay in the East, don't you worry," he said, looking at Daisy and then back at me. "I'd be a fool to live anywhere else."

At that moment, Miss Baker spoke up: "Absolutely!" It was the first thing she had said since I entered the room. It surprised both of us. She yawned and stretched.

"I'm stiff," she complained. "I've been lying on that sofa for forever."

"Don't blame me," Daisy replied. "I've been trying to get you to New York all afternoon."

"No, thanks," Miss Baker declined the four cocktails on the table. "I'm in training."

Her host looked at her in disbelief.

"You are!" He quickly finished his drink. "I have no idea how you manage to get things done."

I gazed at Miss Baker, curious about what sort of things she got done. I enjoyed looking at her. She was slender, with a small chest, and stood with an upright posture, almost like a young cadet. Her gray, sun-strained eyes looked back at me with polite curiosity. Her face had a delicate charm, mixed with a hint of boredom. It suddenly occurred to me that I had seen her, or a picture of her, somewhere before.

"You live in West Egg," she said sympathetically. "I know someone there."

"I don't know anyone—" I began.

"You must know Gatsby."

"Gatsby?" asked Daisy, puzzled. "Who's Gatsby?"

Before I could explain that he was my neighbor, they announced that dinner was ready. Tom Buchanan guided me out of the room, as if he were moving a game piece on a board.

Elegantly and lazily, the two young women walked ahead of us. The porch was bathed in a rosy hue from the sunset. Four flickering candles were on the table, their flames swaying in the gentle breeze.

"Why candles?" Daisy questioned. "In two weeks, it'll be the longest day of the year." She looked at all of us with a bright smile. "Do you always look forward to the longest day of the year and then miss it? I always do."

"We should plan something," Miss Baker stated, yawning.

"Alright," said Daisy. "What should we plan?" She turned to me, seeking assistance. "What do people usually plan?"

Before I could respond, her eyes fixated on her injured little finger, filled with a mixture of awe and pain.

"Look!" she complained. "I hurt it."

We all glanced at her finger. The knuckle was bruised.

"You did it, Tom," she accused. "I know you didn't mean to, but you did it. That's what I get for marrying a man who's a hulking specimen—"

"I dislike the word 'hulking,' " Tom objected. "Even jokingly."

"Hulking," Daisy insisted.

Sometimes Daisy and Miss Baker talked at once. Their conversations were as cool and detached as their white dresses. They both accepted the presence of Tom and me, making polite but minimal efforts to entertain or be entertained. They understood that dinner would eventually end, followed by the evening itself, which would be put away without much thought. This was a stark contrast to the fast-paced West.

"You make me feel uncultured, Daisy," I confessed, sipping on my second glass of red wine. "Can't we talk about something else?"

I didn't have any specific topic in mind with that remark, but it sparked an unexpected response.

"Civilization is falling apart," Tom burst out angrily. "I've become a pessimist about everything. Have you read The Rise of the Black Empires by Goddard?"

"No, I haven't," I replied, taken aback by his tone.

"Well, it's a great book that everyone should read. The idea is that if we're not careful, the white race will be completely erased. It's all based on science. It's been proven."

"Tom's becoming quite thoughtful," Daisy interjected, looking bored. "He reads these deep books with long words in them. What was that word we were...?"

"Well, these books are all scientific," Tom insisted. "This author has figured it all out. We have to be alert or these other races will take control."

"We have to stop them," Daisy whispered, squinting fiercely at the intense sun.

"You should live in California—" Miss Baker started to say, but Tom cut her off by shifting heavily in his seat.

"The idea is that we're Nordics. I am, and you are, and you are," he said, pausing briefly before including Daisy with a slight nod. She winked at me again. "And we've created everything that contributes to civilization—science, art, and all that. Can you understand?"

There was something pitiful in his intense focus. When the telephone rang inside shortly after and the butler left the porch, Daisy took advantage and leaned toward me.

"I'll tell you a secret about the butler," she whispered excitedly. "It's about his nose. Do you want to hear?"

"That's why I'm here."

"Well, he wasn't always a butler. He used to polish silver for some people in New York who had a large silver set for two hundred people. He polished it all day long, and eventually it started to affect his nose—"

"Things went from bad to worse," Miss Baker suggested.

19 "Yes. Things went from bad to worse, until finally he had to give up his position."

For a moment, I listened intently. Then the sunlight faded, but slowly, like a child who doesn't want the day to end.

The butler returned and whispered something to Tom, who frowned, pushed his chair back. He went inside. Daisy immediately tightened up, but she leaned forward once again, her voice filled with warmth and melody.

"I enjoy having you at my table, Nick. You remind me of...of a beautiful rose, absolutely radiant. Don't you agree?" She turned to Miss Baker, seeking confirmation. "A radiant rose?"

This was not true. I do not resemble a rose in the slightest. Daisy was merely improvising. However, her words carried a captivating warmth, as if her heart was secretly trying to reach out. Quickly though, she threw her napkin on the table, excused herself, and hurried into the house.

Miss Baker and I exchanged a quick glance, without any meaningful communication. I was about to speak when she hushed me. We could hear muffled conversation inside, prompting Miss Baker to lean forward and eavesdrop. The discussion seemed to be energetic and then stopped very quickly.

"He's got some woman in New York," Miss Baker whispered urgently.

I stared at her, puzzled. "What do you mean?"

"Tom's seeing someone else," she explained, surprised that I didn't already know.

"Oh," I said, finally understanding. "She shouldn't call him during dinner, should she?"

Before I could fully process her words, I heard the sound of footsteps and a rustle of clothing. Tom and Daisy returned to the table.

"There's nothing we could do," Daisy said, forcing a cheerful tone.

She sat down, giving Miss Baker and me a quick glance before speaking again. "I stepped outside for a moment, and it's so enchanting out there. I heard a bird on the lawn. It's singing its heart out," she trilled. "Isn't it romantic, Tom?"

"Very romantic," he mumbled, looking miserable. Then, he turned to me and added, "If it's still light enough after dinner, I want to show you the stables."

The phone rang loudly again inside, startling everyone. Daisy shook her head firmly at Tom. Table talk faded away, leaving only fragments of the last few minutes. The candles were lit again, although it seemed pointless. I wanted to look directly at everyone, yet at the same time, I wanted to avoid their gaze. I couldn't guess what Daisy and Tom were thinking. Even Miss Baker couldn't ignore the phone's ringing as a fifth guest. Some might be excited by this kind of thing, but I felt like calling the cops.

Needless to say, the topic of the horses was not brought up again. Tom and Miss Baker walked back to the library. I followed Daisy to the front porch, pretending to be interested. We sat together on her wicker furniture.

Daisy cradled her face in her hands, feeling its beautiful shape. Her eyes wandered into the dark night. It was clear that strong emotions consumed her. I asked some calming questions about her daughter.

"We don't know each other well, Nick," she suddenly remarked. "Even though we're cousins. You didn't come to my wedding."

"I hadn't returned from the war."

"That's true." She paused. "Well, I've had a really tough time, Nick. I have a bad outlook on many things."

Clearly, she had good reason to feel that way. I waited for her to say more, but after a moment, I instead brought up the topic of her daughter.

"I guess she talks and eats, right?"

"Oh, yes." She looked distractedly at me. "Listen, Nick. Let me tell you what I said when she was born. She was less than an hour old, and Tom was nowhere to be found. I woke up with a terrible feeling and asked the nurse if it was a boy or a girl. She told me it was a girl, so I turned my head away and cried. 'Alright,' I said, 'I'm glad it's a girl. And I hope she'll be foolish—that's the best thing a girl can be in this world, a beautiful little fool.'

"You see, I think everything is awful regardless," she continued with a firm attitude. "I know. I've been everywhere, seen everything, and done everything." Her eyes darted around, somewhat like Tom's, and she laughed with in a way that showed her discontent. "Sophisticated—God, I'm sophisticated!"

As soon as her voice stopped, I could tell she was feeling serious. It made me uneasy, as if she was trying to get an emotional response from me. I waited, and soon enough, she looked at me with a smug expression on her beautiful face like she was part of some secret snobby society.

～

INSIDE, the red room glowed with light. Tom and Miss Baker sat at opposite ends of the long couch. She read aloud to him from the Saturday Evening Post. The lamplight glimmered along the pages as she turned them, her slender arm muscles flexing.

When we entered, she silenced us momentarily with a raised hand.

"To be continued," she announced, tossing the magazine onto the table, "in the next issue. It's ten o'clock," she noted, seemingly noticing the time on the ceiling. "Time for this proper young lady to go to bed."

"Jordan is going to play in the tournament tomorrow," Daisy explained, "over at Westchester."

"Oh—so you're Jordan Baker."

I now understood why her face was familiar. It had appeared in numerous photographs of the lively social scene in Asheville, Hot Springs, and Palm Beach. I had also heard some awful story about her, but I had forgotten the specifics.

"Good night," she said softly to Daisy. "Please wake me up at eight."

"If you promise to get up."

"I will. Good night, Mr. Carraway. See you soon."

"Of course you will," Daisy confirmed. "In fact, I might even arrange a marriage. Visit us often, Nick, and I'll bring you two together."

"Good night," Miss Baker called from the stairs. "I didn't hear a thing."

"She's a nice girl," Tom remarked after a moment. "They shouldn't let her wander around the country like this."

"Who shouldn't?" Daisy asked coldly.

"Her family."

"Her family consists only of an elderly aunt. Besides, Nick is going to take care of her, right, Nick? She'll be spending many weekends here this summer. I think the influence of a stable home will be good for her."

Daisy and Tom looked at each other silently for a moment.

"Is she from New York?" I asked quickly.

"No, she's from Louisville. We spent our childhood together there."

"Did you have a little heart-to-heart talk with Nick on the porch?" Tom interrupted suddenly.

25 "Do you remember if we had that talk?" Daisy asked me, her face filled with uncertainty. "I can't seem to recall, but I think we discussed the Nordic race. Yes, I'm pretty sure we did—"

"Don't believe everything you hear, Nick," Tom warned me.

I casually mentioned that I hadn't heard anything at all. It was time to leave and as I started my car, Daisy abruptly called out, "Wait!"

"I forgot to ask you something, and it's important. We heard that you were engaged to a girl out West."

"That's correct," Tom confirmed. "We heard about your engagement."

"It's a false rumor. I'm too poor."

"But we heard it," Daisy insisted, surprising me as she opened up like a blooming flower. "We heard it from three different people, so it must be true."

Of course, I understood what they were referring to, but I wasn't even remotely engaged. The fact that gossip had spread the news was one of the reasons I had come to the East. You can't end a friendship just because of rumors, and on the other hand, I had no intention of being talked into a marriage I didn't want.

26 Their curiosity touched me and made them seem less distant in their wealth. However, I felt confused and somewhat disgusted as I drove away. It seemed to me that Daisy should have immediately left the house with her child in her arms due to this other woman of Tom's. But apparently, she had no such intention in mind. As for Tom, the fact that he had some woman in New York was not as surprising as the fact that he had been affected by a book. It seemed

like he was now exploring stale ideas instead of relying on his own confident nature.

It was already mid-summer. When I arrived home in West Egg, I parked the car in the shed and looked out into the yard. The trees blew in the breeze. As I turned to watch the silhouette of a cat moving across the moonlight, I realized I was not alone. Standing about fifty feet away was a figure who had emerged from the shadow of my neighbor's mansion. Hands in pockets, he gazed at the silver pepper of the stars. The calmness of his movements and the confident stance he had on the lawn made it clear that it was Mr. Gatsby himself, perhaps trying to ascertain his place in our local world.

I decided to approach him. Earlier at dinner, Miss Baker had mentioned him, so I figured that would serve as an introduction. However, I refrained from calling out to him, as he showed a sudden indication that he preferred to be by himself. He extended his arms towards the dark water in an unusual manner, and even though I was far from him, I could have sworn that he was shaking. Without meaning to, I glanced towards the sea--but there was nothing to be seen except for a small, distant green light that could have been the end of a dock. When I turned my gaze back to search for Gatsby, he had disappeared, and I found myself alone once more in the restless darkness.

CHAPTER

TWO

28   Between West Egg and New York, the road quickly runs along the railroad. At this point, there is a desolate area is known as the valley of ashes. It's a strange farm where ashes grow into hills. The ashes cover the houses, chimneys, rising smoke, and even men who work in the powdery air. Sometimes, a line of gray train cars slowly creep and creak as they come to a stop. Immediately, the ash-colored men swarm around with heavy shovels, stirring up a dense cloud. It's hard to see what they're doing.

Above the ash, you will eventually notice the piercing gaze of Doctor T. J. Eckleburg, which are on a billboard. His eyes are a vibrant blue and incredibly large. These eyes seem to peer out from nowhere, as they are framed by enormous yellow spectacles that rest on an imaginary nose. It appears that an eye doctor placed this ad there to attract more patients in the borough of Queens, yet disappeared. Nevertheless, those eyes, slightly faded, continue to watch over the dumping ground.

29   The valley of ashes is an unpleasant area located next to a dirty river. Sometimes, when the drawbridge is up, train passengers have no choice but to look at the depressing scene for up to thirty

minutes. Trains usually stop there for at least a minute. That's how I ended up meeting Tom Buchanan's mistress for the first time.

Everyone made a big deal about Tom having a mistress. People didn't like seeing him in popular cafes with her. I was curious, but I didn't really want to meet her. One afternoon, I went to New York with Tom on the train. When we stopped near the ash-heaps, Tom suddenly stood up and forcefully pulled me out of the car.

"We're getting off," he insisted. "I want you to meet my girl."

I think he was quite drunk from lunch. He was determined to have my company, almost to the point of being aggressive. He seemed to assume that I had nothing better to do on a Sunday afternoon.

I trailed behind him as we crossed a short fence by the railroad tracks, and we strolled back along the road while the eyes of Doctor Eckleburg secretly observed us. The only structure in sight was a small yellow brick building. It was like a little Main Street, but without very much. Two of the three shops inside were either vacant or closed, and the remaining one was an auto garage called "Repairs. George B. Wilson. Cars bought and sold." Intrigued, I followed Tom inside.

Upon entering, I noticed that the interior appeared bleak and unsuccessful. The only automobile visible was a dusty Ford wreck. I couldn't help but wonder if this small garage was a front, concealing luxurious and romantic apartments above it. Just as I entertained this thought, the owner emerged from an office, wiping his hands with a piece of cloth. He was a pale, lackluster man, somewhat attractive but lacking of vitality. A glimmer of hope appeared in his light blue eyes when he noticed our presence.

"Hello, Wilson, my friend," Tom greeted him cheerfully, patting him on the shoulder. "How's business?"

"I can't complain," Wilson replied unconvincingly. "When are you going to sell me that car?"

"Next week. My man is currently working on it," Tom answered.

"He seems to be working quite slowly, doesn't he?" Wilson commented.

"No, he doesn't," Tom responded coldly. "And if that's how you feel, perhaps I should consider selling it elsewhere."

"I didn't mean that," Wilson explained quickly. "I just meant—"

His voice trailed off and Tom looked around the garage impatiently. Then I heard footsteps on the stairs, and a moment later, a slightly thick woman stood in the office doorway, blocking out the light. She was in her mid-thirties and shapely. She wasn't exceptionally beautiful, but there was a noticeable energy about her, as if her body was always buzzing with excitement. She smiled slowly and, walking through her husband as if he were invisible. She shook hands with Tom, looking him directly in the eyes. Then she licked her lips and, without turning around, spoke to her husband in a soft, coarse voice:

"Get some chairs, will you? So someone can sit down."

"Oh, of course," Wilson agreed hurriedly and headed towards the small office. His wife, who moved closer to Tom.

"I need to talk to you," Tom said. "Catch the next train."

"Alright."

"I'll meet you by the newsstand on the lower level."

She nodded and moved away from him, just as George Wilson emerged from his office door with two chairs.

We waited for her further down the road, out of sight. It was a few days before the Fourth of July, and a young, skinny Italian child was placing firecrackers in a line along the railroad track.

"This place is horrible, isn't it?" Tom commented, exchanging a disapproving look with Doctor Eckleburg. "Getting away is good for her."

"Doesn't her husband mind?"

"Wilson? He thinks she goes to visit her sister in New York. He doesn't know anything."

So Tom Buchanan, his girlfriend, and I traveled together to New York—well, not exactly together, as Mrs. Wilson sat in a separate car.

In New York, she changed into a brown patterned dress that clung tightly to her slightly wide hips, then Tom assisted her onto the platform. At the newsstand, she purchased a copy of Town Tattle and a magazine about movies. In the station drugstore, she bought some cold cream and a small bottle of perfume. Upstairs, in the dim and echoing driveway, she watched four taxis drive away before she chose a new one. It was lavender-colored with gray seats, and we smoothly moved away from the busy station and into the bright sunlight. But then she suddenly turned towards the window and, leaning forward, tapped on the front glass.

"I really want to get one of those dogs," she said earnestly. "I want to have one for the apartment. They're so nice to have—a dog."

We stood behind an elderly man with gray hair. He had a basket hanging from his neck that held twelve adorable puppies of various breeds.

"What kind of dogs are they?" Mrs. Wilson asked eagerly, leaning towards the man at the taxi window.

"They're all sorts of breeds. What kind are you looking for, ma'am?" he replied.

"I'd love to have one of those police dogs. Do you happen to have any?" she inquired.

The man peered into the basket and carefully picked up one of the squirming puppies by the back of its neck.

"That's not a police dog," Tom stated.

"No, it's not exactly a police dog," the man replied, sounding disappointed. "It's more like an Airedale." He ran his hand over the puppy's brown back. "Look at that coat. It's quite impressive. This dog won't give you any trouble."

"I think it's adorable," Mrs. Wilson exclaimed enthusiastically. "How much does it cost?"

"Ten dollars for this dog," the man replied, looking at it with admiration. "But let me tell you, it's worth it."

The Airedale, which definitely had some Airedale traits even though its white feet were surprising, changed owners and settled comfortably in Mrs. Wilson's lap. She lovingly stroked its weather-proof coat.

"Is it a boy or a girl?" she asked delicately.

"That dog? It's a boy," the man answered.

"It's a girl," Tom declared confidently. "Take your money and go buy ten more dogs."

We drove to Fifth Avenue, which felt warm and peaceful on that Sunday afternoon. It almost seemed like we were in a countryside setting, and I half expected to see a large herd of white sheep turning the corner.

"Wait a moment," I said, "I have to leave you here."

"No, you can't," Tom interrupted. "Myrtle will be upset if you don't come up to the apartment. Right, Myrtle?"

"Come on," she urged. "I'll call my sister Catherine. People who know her say she's incredibly beautiful."

"Well, I would like to, but..."

We continued on, cutting through the park and heading towards the residential area. The cab stopped at 158th Street, at one of the many apartment buildings. Mrs. Wilson took a proud look around the neighborhood. She felt good about herself and took the dog into the building.

"I'm going to invite the McKees to come up," she announced as we got into the elevator. "And, of course, I have to call my sister too."

The apartment was on the top floor, and it had a small living room, dining room, bedroom, and bathroom. The living room was very cluttered because the furniture was too big for the space. It was hard to walk around without tripping over chairs with scenes of women swinging in the gardens of Versailles. The only artwork was a large photograph that looked like a blurry rock with a hen on it. However, if you looked closely, the blurry rock turned into a hat and the face of a happy old lady filled the room. On the table were some old issues of Town Tattle, a book called Simon Called Peter, and some gossip magazines from Broadway. Mrs. Wilson's first priority was taking care of her dog. She asked the elevator boy to bring a box of straw and some milk. The elevator boy also added a tin of big, hard dog biscuits, one of which sat in the saucer of milk all afternoon, slowly falling apart. Meanwhile, Tom pulled out a bottle of whiskey from a locked cabinet.

I've been drunk only twice in my life, and the second time was that afternoon. So everything that happened has a blurry, unclear quality to it, although the apartment was filled with bright sunlight until after eight o'clock. Mrs. Wilson sat on Tom's lap and made phone calls to several people. Then, we realized we didn't have any cigarettes, so I left to buy some at the drugstore on the corner. When I returned, both Mrs. Wilson and Tom had disappeared, so I discreetly sat down in the living room and read a chapter of Simon Called Peter. Either the book was terrible or the whiskey made everything seem strange, because I couldn't make any sense of it.

Just as Tom and Myrtle (after the first drink, Mrs. Wilson and I called each other by our first names) reappeared, more people started arriving at the apartment door.

Catherine, Tom's sister, was a slim, sophisticated woman in her thirties. She had short, red hair and a face that was powdered very pale. Her eyebrows had been plucked and drawn back on at a sharper angle, but they looked kind of blurred. Every time she moved, the numerous pottery bracelets on her arms made a constant clicking sound. She came into the apartment as if she owned it, looking possessively at the furniture, which made me wonder if she lived there. But when I asked her, she burst into laughter, repeated my question out loud, and told me she actually lived with a girl friend at a hotel.

The man named Mr. McKee was a pale and delicate-looking individual who lived in the apartment below. He appeared to have just finished shaving, as there was still a white spot of shaving cream on his cheekbone. He greeted everyone in the room with great respect. He later informed me that he was involved in the "artistic field," and I later learned that he worked as a photographer. On the wall, the large, blurry photograph of Mrs. Wilson's mother was one which Mr. McKee had taken.

Mr. McKee's wife was loud, tired-looking, attractive, and unpleasant. She proudly mentioned that her husband had taken her picture 127 times since they got married.

Mrs. Wilson had changed her outfit earlier and was now wearing an intricate cream-colored chiffon dress that made constant rustling sounds as she moved around the room. Her change in appearance seemed to bring about a change in her personality as well. The energetic liveliness she had displayed earlier in the garage was now transformed into an imposing sense of superiority. Her laughter, gestures, and statements became increasingly affected with each passing moment. As she grew more animated, the room seemed to shrink around her, and she appeared to be spinning on a creaky pivot through the smoky air.

In a loud, artificial voice, she exclaimed to her sister, "Most of these fellas will always try to cheat you. Money is all they care about. Last week, I had a woman come up here to examine my feet, and when she gave me the bill, you would have thought she had performed surgery on my appendix!"

Mrs. McKee inquired, "What was the name of that woman?"

"I must say, I really like your dress," Mrs. McKee complimented. "I think it's adorable."

Mrs. Wilson dismissed the compliment with a raised eyebrow. "It's just a crazy, old thing. I only wear it when I don't care how I look."

"But it looks stunning on you, if you know what I mean," Mrs. McKee persisted.

We all fell silent, observing Mrs. Wilson. She brushed a strand of hair away from her eyes and smiled brightly at us.

After a moment, Mr. McKee said, "I'd love to get a photo of you in that dress. I should adjust the lighting. I want to bring out the sculptural aspects of your features. And I would attempt to capture all the intricacies of your hairstyle."

"I wouldn't even think of changing the lighting," Mrs. McKee protested. "I think it's--"

Her husband interrupted her with a "Shh!" and we all refocused our attention on Mrs. Wilson. At that moment, Tom Buchanan let out a loud yawn and stood up.

"You McKees should get some drinks," he suggested. "Get more ice and mineral water, Myrtle, before everyone falls asleep."

"I already told that boy about the ice," Myrtle said with an exasperated expression, reflecting her disappointment in the irresponsibility of the lower classes. "These people! You have to constantly remind them."

She looked at me and laughed for no reason. Then she walked over to the dog, kissed it happily, and went into the kitchen. She acted like a team of chefs was waiting there to fulfill her every order.

"I've done some impressive things out on Long Island," said Mr. McKee confidently.

Tom stared at him with confusion.

"We have two of them on display downstairs."

"What two things?" asked Tom.

"Two paintings. I call one of them Montauk Point—The Gulls, and the other Montauk Point—The Sea."

Catherine, the sister, sat down next to me on the couch.

"Do you also live on Long Island?" she asked me.

"I live in West Egg."

"Really? I attended a party there about a month ago. It was at a man named Gatsby's house. Do you know him?"

"I live next door to him."

"Well, they say he's a relative of Kaiser Wilhelm's. That's where all his money comes from."

"Really?"

She nodded. "I'm afraid of him. I wouldn't want him to have anything against me."

This interesting information about my neighbor was interrupted by Mrs. McKee suddenly pointing at Catherine:

"Chester, I think you could do something with her," she exclaimed, but Mr. McKee only nodded, bored, and turned his attention to Tom.

"I would love to do more work on Long Island if I could get my foot in the door. All I'm asking for is an opportunity."

"Ask Myrtle," said Tom, breaking into a burst of laughter as Mrs. Wilson came in with a tray. "She'll give you a letter of introduction, won't you, Myrtle?"

"Do what?" she asked, startled.

Catherine leaned in and whispered to me:

"Neither of them can stand their spouses. What I'm saying is, why continue living with them if they can't stand them? If I were them, I'd get a divorce and marry each other right away."

"Doesn't she like Wilson either?"

The response to this question was unexpected. Myrtle, who had overheard, erupted.

"You see," Catherine exclaimed triumphantly. She whispered again. "It's actually his wife who's keeping them apart. She's a Catholic, and they don't believe in divorce."

Daisy was not a Catholic, and I was a little taken aback by the lie.

"When they do get married," Catherine continued, "they plan to move out West for a while until things settle down."

"It would be better to go to Europe."

The sky outside the window shimmered. Suddenly, Mrs. McKee's loud voice called me back into reality.

"I almost made a mistake too," she declared vigorously. "I almost married a man who had been pursuing me for years. I knew he wasn't on my level. Everyone kept telling me: 'Lucille, that man is way beneath you!' But luckily, I met Chester and he saved me."

"Yes, but listen," Myrtle Wilson interjected. "At least you didn't marry him."

"I know I didn't," Mrs. McKee confirmed.

"Well, I did," Myrtle confessed. "And that's the difference between your situation and mine." Myrtle took a moment to think.

"I married him because I believed he was a true gentleman," she finally answered. "I thought he had good breeding, but he turned out to be unworthy of even cleaning my shoes."

"You were infatuated with him for a while," Catherine reminded her.

"Infatuated with him!" Myrtle exclaimed. "Who said I was infatuated with him? I was no more infatuated with him than I am with that man over there."

She suddenly pointed at me, and everyone looked at me with accusatory eyes. I tried to show through my expression that I didn't expect any affection.

"The only mistake I made was when I married him. I knew right away that it was a mistake. He borrowed someone's best suit to wear for the wedding, and he never even told me about it. Then one day, the man came to collect it when he was out. 'Oh, is that your suit?' I said. 'This is the first I've heard of it.' But I gave it to him, and then I just cried all afternoon."

"She really should leave him," Catherine said to me. "They've been living above that garage for eleven years, and Tom is the first sweetheart she's ever had."

The bottle of whiskey, a second one, was now in constant demand by everyone except Catherine, who claimed she felt just as good without it. Tom called the janitor and asked him to bring some famous sandwiches, which were a complete meal on their own. I wanted to leave and take a walk toward the park in the soft twilight, but every time I tried, I became caught up in a loud argument that pulled me back into my chair as if I were tied down. But high above the city, our row of lit windows must have added to the allure of the streets at dusk, and I saw a person outside looking up and wondering. I was both intrigued and repelled by the endless variety of life, feeling both inside and outside of it all at once.

Myrtle moved her chair closer to mine, and then she began to recount her first encounter with Tom.

"It happened on the two small seats facing each other that are always the last ones available on the train. I was traveling to New York to visit my sister and stay the night. Tom was dressed in a fancy suit and shiny shoes, and I couldn't take my eyes off him. But whenever he glanced at me, I had to pretend I was reading the advertisement above his head. When we arrived at the station, he stood right beside me, with his pristine shirt pressing against my arm. So, in a fit of nerves, I falsely claimed that I would call a police officer, although deep down, he knew I was lying. I was so thrilled and anxious that when I got into a taxi with him, I almost mistook it for a subway train. The only thought repeating in my head was, 'You can't live forever. You can't live forever.'"

She turned to Mrs. McKee and forced out a fake laugh that filled the room.

"Oh darling," she exclaimed, "once I'm done with this dress, I'll give it to you. Tomorrow, I must get another one. I need to create a list of all the things I have to get. A massage and a stylish hairdo, a collar for my dog, one of those adorable ashtrays with a spring mechanism, and a lovely wreath with a black silk bow for my mother's grave that will last throughout the summer. I got to jot down a list so I won't forget all the things I got to do."

At around nine o'clock, I glanced at my watch and realized that an hour had already passed. Mr. McKee had dozed off in a chair, his hands clenched tightly in his lap, as if he were a daring man captured in a photograph. I took out my handkerchief and gently wiped away a dried spot of shaving cream that had been bothering me on his cheek all afternoon.

The small dog sat on the table, its eyes clouded and unseeing, occasionally letting out soft groans. People would appear and then disappear, make plans to go somewhere, and then lose each other, only to search and find each other a few steps away. Sometime close to midnight, Tom Buchanan and Mrs. Wilson confronted each other, their voices filled with intense passion, debating whether Mrs. Wilson had the right to mention Daisy's name.

"Daisy! Daisy! Daisy!" Mrs. Wilson shouted. "I'll say it whenever I want to! Daisy! Dai—"

With a quick and skillful motion, Tom Buchanan struck her nose with the palm of his hand, breaking it.

There were towels stained with blood on the floor of the bathroom, and women's voices scolding each other could be heard over the chaos. Above it all, there was a long, broken cry of pain. Mr. McKee woke up from his nap and stumbled towards the door in a dazed state. He reached the middle of the room and turned back to look at the scene—a scene of his wife and Catherine trying to comfort someone while navigating through the crowded furniture with medical supplies. The figure on the couch, bleeding heavily, was attempting to cover the tapestry scenes of Versailles with a copy of a gossip magazine called Town Tattle. After a moment, Mr. McKee turned again and continued on his way out the door. I grabbed my hat from the chandelier and followed him.

"We should have lunch together sometime," he suggested, as we groaned our way down in the elevator.

"Where should we go?" I asked.

"Anywhere," he replied.

"Don't touch the lever," snapped the elevator boy.

"I apologize," said Mr. McKee with dignity, "I wasn't aware that I was touching it."

"Okay," I agreed, "I'll be happy to go."

"Beauty and the Beast... Loneliness... Old Grocery Horse... Brooklyn Bridge..."

Then, later on, I found myself on the lower level of Pennsylvania Station. I waited for the 4:00PM train.

CHAPTER

THREE

⁴⁶ DURING THE SUMMER NIGHTS, I heard music coming from my neighbor's house. In his beautiful gardens, people moved around like tiny insects, talking softly and enjoying champagne under the sparkling stars. In the afternoon, when the tide was high, I saw his guests jumping into the water from a tall platform, or relaxing on the warm sand of his beach. His two motorboats sliced through the water, creating waves of foam. On weekends, his fancy Rolls-Royce became like a big bus, taking people to and from the city from morning until late at night. By Monday, eight workers, including an extra gardener, worked all day to clean up after the wild party from the night before.

That Friday, five crates filled with oranges and lemons would be delivered from a fruit seller in New York. Over the weekend, the peels from the oranges and lemons would pile up and be discarded. I heard that my neighbor had a fancy juice maker. It needed to be operated by a butler hundreds of time to get enough juice for the parties.

⁴⁷ Every two weeks, a group of caterers arrived at Gatsby's garden with hundreds of feet of canvas and vibrant colored lights. The buffet tables displayed shiny appetizers. Inside the main hall, a bar with a

28

genuine brass railing was set up and stocked with a variety of gins, liquors, and cordials.

By seven o'clock, the full orchestra had arrived. It wasn't just a small ensemble, but a complete group with oboes, trombones, saxophones, viols, cornets, piccolos, and both low and high drums. The last swimmers returned from the beach and were getting ready upstairs. The cars from New York filled the driveway, with groups of five across parked one after another. The bar was busy, and rounds of cocktails flowed. The air was filled with lively conversations, laughter, and carefree remarks.

As the sun sets, the lights in the garden grow brighter. The orchestra, now playing upbeat music, fills the air with excitement. The voices of the guests rise in volume, creating a lively atmosphere. Laughter becomes more frequent and abundant. There are young women, gliding away, excited and victorious, through the ever-changing sea of faces, voices, and vibrant colors illuminated by the shifting lights.

Suddenly, one of these free-spirited girls, dressed in shimmering opal, reaches out and grabs a cocktail, taking a gulp for courage. With her hands moving gracefully like a dancer from San Francisco, she steps onto a platform and starts dancing alone. A momentary hush falls over the crowd, but the orchestra leader adjusts the rhythm to match her movements. Everyone watches and soon people begin saying she is famous. The party has started.

I think back to the first night I went to Gatsby's house and realize I was one of the few guests who received an invitation. At Gatsby's, people didn't receive invitations. They just showed up. They would hop into cars that took them out to Long Island, and somehow they would find themselves at Gatsby's doorstep. Once there, they would be introduced by someone who knew Gatsby. Many times though, they'd come and go without ever having met Gatsby at all.

But I was different. I had actually been invited. On that Saturday morning, a chauffeur wearing a robin's-egg blue uniform walked across my lawn and handed me a surprisingly formal note from his employer. The note stated that it would be Gatsby's honor if I attended his "little party" that night. Gatsby had seen me on several occasions and had intended to visit me much earlier, but circumstances beyond his control had prevented it. The note was signed by Jay Gatsby himself, written in a grand and majestic hand.

Dressed in white, I went over to his yard a little after seven. I was immediately struck by the presence of young British men scattered about. They all dressed nicely, all seeming a little eager, and all speaking quietly to successful and wealthy Americans. I was certain that they were trying to sell something: bonds, insurance, or cars. They knew they were among the wealthy.

As soon as I arrived, I tried to find the host. No one seemed to know where he was. Feeling defeated, I walked over to the cocktail table. It was the only spot in the garden where a single person could stand without appearing awkward.

I was about to drink heavily out of sheer embarrassment when Jordan Baker emerged from the house and stood at the top of the steps. Again, she had a bored expression.

Whether I was invited or not, I realized I needed to attach myself to someone before I could start being friendly to those passing by.

"Hello!" I called out, approaching her. My voice echoed strangely across the garden.

"I thought you might be here," she said absentmindedly as I approached. "I remembered that you lived next door to..."

She held my hand, but promised to return to me in a moment. Two girls approached her.

"Hello!" they both exclaimed. "Sorry you didn't win."

They were referring to the golf tournament. She had lost in the finals the week before.

"You probably don't remember us," one of the girls in yellow said, "but we met you here about a month ago."

They spoke for a moment as I watched the waiters bringing drinks to guests.

"Do you come to these parties often?" Jordan asked the girl beside her.

"The last one was the party where I first met you," the girl replied with an alert, self-assured voice. She turned to her companion and asked, "Wasn't it for you, Lucille?"

It was indeed for Lucille as well.

"I enjoy attending these parties," Lucille said with a carefree tone. "I don't really mind what I do, so I always have a good time. The last time I was here and I tore my dress. I was sent a new one the next week."

"Did you keep it?" Jordan asked.

"Of course I did. I was planning to wear it tonight. It was too big in the bust and needed alterations. It was a gas blue dress with lavender beads. It cost two hundred and sixty-five dollars."

"There's something strange about a guy who would do something like that," the other girl eagerly commented. "He must really not want any trouble with anyone."

"Who are we talking about?" I asked.

"Gatsby. Someone told me—"

The two girls and Jordan leaned in closer, speaking in a hushed and secretive manner.

"Somebody told me they believed he once killed a man."

A thrill ran through all of us. The three men named Mr. Mumble leaned forward, eager to listen.

"I don't think that's the case," Lucille objected skeptically. "I think it's more likely that he was a German spy during the war."

One of the men nodded in agreement.

"I heard that from someone who knew everything about him, someone who grew up with him in Germany," he confidently assured us.

"Oh, no," said the first girl, "that can't be true because he served in the American army during the war." As we switched our belief back to her, she leaned forward with enthusiasm. "Sometimes, when he thinks nobody is watching, you can see it in his eyes. I bet he's killed someone."

53 She narrowed her eyes and shivered. We all looked around for Gatsby.

The first dinner was now being served. Jordan invited me to join her group, who was sitting at a table on the opposite side of the garden. There were three married couples and Jordan's companion, an annoying college student, who was after her.

"Let's leave," Jordan whispered, after a somewhat pointless thirty minutes. "This is overdone."

We stood up, and she explained that we were going to find the host. I had never met him before, she said, which was making me feel uneasy. The college student nodded in a cynical, sad way.

54 The bar, which was the first place we looked, was crowded, but Gatsby wasn't there. Lucille couldn't see him from the top of the stairs, and he wasn't on the porch. On a chance, we tried a door that seemed important, and we walked into a fancy library with Gothic decorations. It looked like it had been taken from an old ruin somewhere overseas.

A plump, middle-aged man, wearing large owl-eyed glasses was sitting somewhat drunk at a big table. He stared unsteadily at the shelves of books. When we walked in, he turned to us, excited.

"What do you think?" he asked urgently.

"About what?"

He gestured towards the bookshelves. "About that. Actually, you don't need to find out. I already did. They're real."

"The books?"

He nodded.

"Absolutely real—they have pages and everything. I thought they might be made of sturdy cardboard. But no, they're definitely real. Pages and everything. Let me show you."

Assuming we were skeptical, he quickly went to the bookcases and came back with Volume One of the Stoddard Lectures.

"See!" he exclaimed triumphantly. "It's a genuine printed book.

It fooled me. This guy is a true master. It's a triumph. Such attention to detail! So realistic! He even knew when to stop, didn't cut the pages. But what more could you want? What do you expect?”

He grabbed the book from me and quickly put it back on the shelf, muttering that if one brick was removed, the whole library could collapse.

“Who brought you here?” he asked. “Or did you just come on your own? I was brought here. Most people were brought.”

Jordan looked at him attentively, cheerfully, without responding.

“I was brought here by a woman named Roosevelt,” he continued. “Mrs. Claud Roosevelt. Do you know her? I met her somewhere last night. I've been drinking heavily for about a week now, and I thought sitting in a library might sober me up.”

“Has it?”

“A little bit, I think. I can't tell yet. I've only been here for an hour. Did I mention the books? They're real. They're—”

“You already told us.”

We shook hands with him solemnly and returned outside.

There was dancing happening on the canvas in the garden. Older men were pushing young girls in awkward circles, while couples appeared fashionable but uncomfortable in the corners. There were also many single girls dancing by themselves. The excitement grew. A famous singer performed in Italian, followed by a well-known singer performing jazz. In between, people were doing entertaining things all over the garden, causing laughter to fill the summer sky. Two twins who were stage performers did a comedy act. The moon shimmered on the water.

I was sitting with Jordan Baker at a table, but watched all that was going on around us. We were seated with a man and a young girl.

During a break in the entertainment, the man looked at me and smiled politely.

“You look familiar,” he said. “Were you in the military during the war?”

"Yes, I was in the Twenty-eighth Infantry," I replied.

"I served in the Sixteenth military division until June nineteen-eighteen. I had a feeling that I had seen you before."

We chatted for a moment about some small, dull villages in France. It seemed that he lived nearby because he mentioned that he had recently purchased a hydroplane and planned to test it out in the morning.

"Would you like to join me, old friend? We'll stay near the shore along the Sound."

"What time?"

"Whenever works best for you."

I almost asked his name, but then Jordan looked over and smiled.

"Having a good time now?" she asked.

"Much better." I turned back to my new acquaintance. "This is an unusual party for me. I haven't even met the host. I live over there—" I gestured towards the hidden hedge in the distance, "and this man Gatsby sent his driver with an invitation."

For a moment, he looked at me as if he did not understand.

"I am Gatsby," he suddenly said.

"What!" I exclaimed. "Oh, I apologize."

"I thought you knew, old friend. I'm afraid I'm not a very good host."

He smiled in an understanding way--more than understanding, actually. It was one of those rare smiles that makes you feel reassured forever. You may only encounter this kind of smile four or five times in your life. It appeared to face the entire eternal world for a moment and then focused on you with an undeniable bias in your favor. It understood you just as much as you wanted to be understood, believed in you in the way you wanted to believe in yourself, and assured you that it had the exact impression of you that you hoped to portray at your very best. Right at that moment, the smile disappeared and I was looking at a stylish young man, slightly rough around the edges, who was a year or two over thirty. His overly formal way of speaking was almost ridiculous. Even before he introduced himself, I had the strong feeling that he was carefully choosing his words.

Just as Mr. Gatsby revealed his identity, a butler hurried toward him and informed him that there was a call for him from Chicago. He excused himself with a slight bow that included each one of us.

"If you need anything, just ask for it, old friend," he insisted, addressing me. "Excuse me, I will rejoin you later."

Once he was gone, I turned immediately to Jordan, feeling compelled to express my surprise. I had expected Mr. Gatsby to be a chubby, mature person in his middle years.

"Who is he?" I asked. "Do you know?"

"He's just a man named Gatsby."

"Where is he from, I mean? And what does he do?"

"Now that we're on the subject," she replied with a tired smile. "Well, he once told me he went to Oxford. Although, I don't believe him."

"Why not?"

"I don't know," she insisted. "I just have a feeling he didn't go there."

Her tone reminded me of the other girl's comment about him killing a man, arousing my curiosity. I would have unquestionably accepted the information that Gatsby came from the swamps of Louisiana or the lower East Side of New York. That made sense to me. But young men didn't, as far as I knew, casually appear out of nowhere and buy a mansion on Long Island Sound.

"Anyway, he throws large parties and I like them. They feel so personal. There's no privacy at small parties."

Suddenly, the music boomed.

"Ladies and gentlemen," he announced. "As requested by Mr. Gatsby, we will now perform Mr. Vladmir Tostoff's latest composition, which caused quite a stir at Carnegie Hall last May. If you read the news, you know it created quite a sensation." He grinned with friendly superiority and added, "Quite a sensation indeed!" The crowd erupted in laughter.

60   "The piece is known," he concluded lustily, "as 'Vladmir Tostoff's Jazz History of the World!' "

The nature of Mr. Tostoff's composition eluded me, because just as it began my eyes fell on Gatsby, standing alone on the marble steps and looking from one group to another with approving eyes. His tanned skin was drawn attractively tight on his face and his short hair looked as though it were trimmed every day. I could see nothing sinister about him. I wondered if the fact that he was not drinking helped to set him off from his guests, for it seemed to me that he grew more correct as the fraternal hilarity increased. When the "Jazz History of the World" was over, girls were putting their heads on men's shoulders in a puppyish, convivial way, girls were swooning backward playfully into men's arms, even into groups, knowing that someone would stop their falls—but no one swooned backward on Gatsby, and no French bob touched Gatsby's shoulder, and no singing quartets were formed with Gatsby's head for one link.

"I beg your pardon."

Gatsby's butler was suddenly standing beside us.

"Miss Baker?" he inquired. "I beg your pardon, but Mr. Gatsby would like to speak to you alone."

"With me?" she exclaimed in surprise.

"Yes, madame."

61   She stood up slowly, looking surprised, and followed the butler to the house. I noticed that she was wearing her evening dress, like all of her dresses, in a sporty style. There was a lively quality to her movements, as if she had first learned to walk on golf courses during fresh, chilly mornings.

I was by myself, and it was almost two o'clock. I heard confusing, intriguing sounds coming from a long room with many windows that overlooked the terrace. I slipped away from Jordan's friend, who was now having an intense conversation with two chorus girls, and who begged me to join them. Instead, I entered the room.

The large room was filled with people. One of the girls in a yellow dress was playing the piano, while next to her stood a tall, red-haired young lady from a famous chorus, singing a song. She had consumed a significant amount of champagne, and as she sang, she decided, clumsily, that everything was very, very sad. Not only was she singing, but she was also crying. Whenever there was a break in the song, she filled it with gasping, sobbing breaths, and then continued the lyrics with a shaky soprano voice. The tears streamed down her cheeks, although not freely. When they touched her heavily beaded eyelashes, they turned black and moved slowly down her face in dark streams. Someone humorously suggested that she sing the notes on her face, and in response, she threw up her hands, collapsed into a chair, and fell into a deep, drunken sleep.

"She had an argument with a man who claims to be her husband," explained a girl next to me.

I looked around. Most of the remaining women were now arguing with men who were supposed to be their husbands. Some wanted to leave and some wanted to stay.

"Every time he sees that I'm enjoying myself, he wants to go home."

"I've never heard anything so selfish in my life."

"We're always the first ones to leave."

Despite the wives' agreement that such malice was unbelievable, the argument ended in a brief struggle. Both wives were lifted, kicking, into the night.

While I waited for my hat in the hallway, Jordan Baker and Gatsby exited the library together. He was speaking to her, but his enthusiasm quickly turned formal as a few people approached to say their goodbyes.

Jordan's friends were calling her impatiently from the porch, but she paused for a moment to shake hands.

"I just heard the most incredible thing," she whispered. "How long were we in there?"

"Oh, about an hour."

"It was... absolutely incredible," she repeated. "But I promised not to tell, and here I am teasing you." She yawned gracefully in my face. "Please come visit me... Look me up in the phone book."

Feeling somewhat embarrassed that I had stayed so late on my first visit, I joined the remaining guests, gathered around Gatsby. I wanted to apologize for not recognizing him in the garden.

"Don't worry about it," he eagerly told me. "Don't give it another thought, old sport." The familiar phrase didn't feel so familiar anymore. "And don't forget, tomorrow morning at nine o'clock, we're going on a hydroplane."

Then the butler, standing behind him, interjected:

"Philadelphia is on the phone for you, sir."

"Okay, give me a minute. Let them know I'll be there soon... Good night."

"Good night."

"Good night." He smiled—and suddenly it seemed meaningful to be among the last to leave, as if he had wanted it that way all along. "Good night, my friend... Good night."

But as I walked down the steps, I realized that the evening wasn't quite over. Just fifty feet from the door, a dozen car headlights illuminated a strange, chaotic scene. In the ditch next to the road, a new car, missing one wheel, sat upright. It had only left Gatsby's driveway a couple of minutes ago. The wheel had come off because it had hit a wall, which explained the detachment. Several curious chauffeurs were now giving it a lot of attention. However, since they had parked their cars in the middle of the road, the noise from those behind them had been unpleasant and loud, making the scene even more chaotic.

A man in a long coat had gotten out of the wreck and was now standing in the middle of the road, looking at the car, then at the tire, and back at the onlookers in a confused but pleasant way.

"You see!" he explained. "It ended up in the ditch."

This fact astonished him, and I first noticed his genuine wonder and then recognized him—it was the man from Gatsby's library.

"How did it happen?"

He shrugged.

"I know absolutely nothing about cars," he said firmly.

"But how did it happen? Did you crash into the wall?"

"Don't ask me," stated Owl Eyes, trying to distance himself from the situation. "I don't know much about driving, especially at night. It happened, and that's all I know."

"You don't understand," the man confessed. "I wasn't the one driving. There's someone else in the car."

The shock that followed this was expressed through a gasp as the door of the coupé slowly swung open. A messy figure emerged from the wreck, awkwardly feeling the ground with an uncertain dancing shoe.

Blinded by the bright headlights and bewildered by the constant horn honking, the person stood swaying for a moment before noticing the man in the long duster.

"What's the matter?" he asked calmly. "Did we run out of gas?"

"Look!"

Several fingers pointed towards the wrecked car.

"It came off," someone clarified.

He nodded.

"At first, I didn't even realize we had stopped."

A pause. Then, taking a deep breath and straightening his posture, he spoke with determination:

"Do you happen to know where the nearest gas station is?"

At least twelve men, some of them in better circumstances than he, explained to him that the wheel and the car were no longer connected.

"Try backing out," he suggested after a moment. "Put it in reverse."

"But the wheel is off!"

He hesitated.

"It doesn't hurt to try," he said.

The blaring of the horns had reached its peak, and I turned away and made my way across the lawn towards home. I glanced back once. A small sliver of a moon was shining over Gatsby's house, casting a serene glow that prevailed over the laughter and the noise from his lively garden. An unexpected sense of emptiness emanated from the windows and the grand doors, leaving the figure of the host standing on the porch, his hand lifted in a formal farewell.

~

REFLECTING on what I have written so far, I realize that I may have given the impression that these events, spread out over three nights several weeks apart, were the only things occupying my thoughts. On the contrary, they were just ordinary occurrences during a busy summer, and, until much later, they held far less of my attention than my personal matters.

Most of the time, I worked. In the early morning, as the sun rose, I hurried through the crowded streets of lower New York to the Probity Trust. I knew my coworkers well and ate lunch with them in crowded restaurants. There was even a brief romance with a girl from Jersey City who worked in the accounting department. Her brother started giving me unfriendly looks, and we stopped speaking in July when she went on vacation.

For dinner, I usually went to the Yale Club, although it was always the least enjoyable part of my day. Afterward, I would go to the library and spend an hour studying investments and securities. The library remained a peaceful place for me to concentrate. If the evening was pleasant, I would take a leisurely stroll to go back to Pennsylvania Station.

I started to enjoy New York. It was busy and exciting. It was pleasing to stroll up Fifth Avenue, spotting captivating women in the crowd and daydreaming that I would soon enter their lives. Sometimes, in my imagination, I would follow them to their apartments tucked away on hidden streets. They would turn and smile at me before disappearing through their doors into the inviting darkness. However, I occasionally felt a haunting loneliness, and sensed it in others too. Poor, young office workers would hang around in front of shop windows, waiting until it was time for a lonely dinner in a quiet restaurant.

Once again, at eight o'clock, when the dimly lit streets in the Forties were filled with a constant stream of bustling taxis, heading towards the theater district, I felt a heaviness in my heart. Passengers leaned closer to one another inside the taxis as they waited, their voices mingling in song, and there was laughter from jokes I couldn't hear. Cigarettes glowed, forming mysterious circles in the air. Imagining that I, too, was rushing towards the excitement and merriment, I wished them all well.

In the middle of the summer, I came across Jordan Baker again after losing sight of her for a while. Initially, I enjoyed being seen with her because she was a famous golfer and everyone knew her. However, my feelings towards her soon changed. It wasn't exactly love, but rather a gentle curiosity. Behind her bored and haughty demeanor, she was hiding something—just like most mannerisms eventually reveal something, even if they don't at first. One day, during a house-party in Warwick, she left a borrowed car out in the rain with the convertible top down, and then lied about it. In that moment, I recalled the story about her that I couldn't quite remember at Daisy's party. During her first major golf tournament, there was a scandal that almost made it into the newspapers. It was suggested that she had cheated by moving her ball from a bad position during the semifinal round. The incident caused quite a stir but eventually faded away. One of the caddies withdrew his statement, and the only other witness admitted that he may have been mistaken. The incident and Jordan's name had stuck together in my memory.

Jordan Baker intentionally avoided intelligent, shrewd men, and I realized it was because she felt more secure when everyone believed she could never deviate from a certain set of rules. She had a tendency to be dishonest, almost as if it were a part of her nature. She could not stand being in a position of weakness, and so I assume that at a young age, she began using deceitful tactics to maintain her confident façade while still satisfying her physical desires.

To me, her dishonesty wasn't a grave issue. I felt only a casual sense of sympathy before ultimately forgetting about it. It was during the same gathering that we had an interesting conversation about her driving. It began when she passed by some workers so closely that the car's fender brushed a button on one man's coat.

"You're a terrible driver," I objected. "Either you should be more cautious, or you shouldn't drive at all."

"I am cautious," she rebutted.

"No, you're not."

"Well, other people are," she replied nonchalantly.

"What does that have to do with anything?" I questioned.

"They will stay out of my way," she asserted confidently. "It takes two people to cause an accident."

"What if you encountered someone as careless as yourself?"

"I hope I never do," she answered. "I despise careless individuals. That's why I appreciate you."

I studied her eyes, tired from the intense sunlight, as she stared straight ahead. In that moment, I thought I might love her. I first, I knew I had to resolve the complicated situation back home. I had been writing letters once a week, signing them with "Love, Nick." Yet, there was an unspoken agreement that needed to be delicately ended before I could truly be free to be in a relationship with someone else.

It seems that everyone believes they possess at least one important virtue. For me, it's my honesty. I consider myself to be one of the few truly honest individuals I have ever encountered.

CHAPTER
FOUR

 On a Sunday morning, as church bells chimed in the nearby villages, Gatsby's house became lively once again, filled with laughter and merriment.

"He's involved in illegal alcohol trade," commented the young ladies, moving gracefully between the cocktails and the beautifully arranged flowers. "They say he even killed a man who discovered his relation to Von Hindenburg and the devil himself. Darling, hand me a rose and pour me a little more of that exquisite drink in this crystal glass."

Once, I recorded the names of those who frequented Gatsby's house during that summer. It's an aged timetable now, falling apart at the folds, labeled "This schedule in effect July 5th, 1922." Yet, I can still decipher the names written in gray ink, which will offer you a clearer insight into those who enjoyed Gatsby's hospitality and cele-brated him without knowing anything substantial about his background.

From East Egg, there were the Chester Beckers and the Leeches, along with a man named Bunsen, whom I knew from my time at Yale. There was also Doctor Webster Civet, who tragically drowned last summer in Maine. The Hornbeams and the Willie Voltaires attended as well, alongside a whole clan known as the Blackbuck family. They huddled together, noses in the air like goats, expressing disdain for anyone who came close. The Ismays and the Chrysties also made appearances (or rather, Hubert Auerbach and Mrs. Chrystie, wife of Mr. Chrystie). Lastly, there was Edgar Beaver, whose hair supposedly turned completely white on a winter afternoon for no apparent reason.

73   Clarence Endive was from East Egg, I believe. He came only once, wearing white pants, and had a fight with a person named Etty in the garden. From a farther part of the Island came the Cheadles and the O. R. P. Schraeders, and the Stonewall Jackson Abrams of Georgia, and the Fishguards and the Ripley Snells. Snell was there three days before he went to prison, after getting so drunk on the driveway that Mrs. Ulysses Swett's car ran over his right hand. The Dancies came too, and S. B. Whitebait, who was well over sixty, and Maurice A. Flink, and the Hammerheads, and Beluga the person who imports tobacco, and Beluga's girls.

From West Egg came the Poles and the Mulreadys and Cecil Roebuck and Cecil Schoen and Gulick the State senator and Newton Orchid, who controlled Films Par Excellence, and Eckhaust and Clyde Cohen and Don S. Schwartz (the son) and Arthur McCarty, all involved with movies in some way. And the Catlips and the Bembergs and G. Earl Muldoon, brother to the Muldoon who later killed his wife. Da Fontano the promoter came there, and Ed Legros and James B. Ferret (known as "Rot-Gut") and the De Jongs and Ernest Lilly—they came to gamble, and when Ferret wandered into the garden, it meant he had lost all his money and Associated Traction would have to make a profitable move the next day.

74   A man named Klipspringer was there so often that he became known as "the boarder"--I think he didn't have any other home. Among the people from the theater were Gus Waize, Horace O'Donavan, Lester Myer, George Duckweed, and Francis Bull. Also from New York were the Chromes, Backhyssons, Dennickers, Russel Betty,

Corrigans, Kellehers, Dewars, Scullys, S.W. Belcher, Smirkes, and the young Quinns, who are now divorced. There was also Henry L. Palmetto, who sadly took his own life by jumping in front of a subway train in Times Square.

Benny McClenahan always arrived with four girls. Although they were never exactly the same people, they were so similar to each other that it seemed like they had been there before. I have forgotten their names, but I believe they were Jaqueline, Consuela, Gloria, Judy, or June. Their last names were either beautiful names of flowers and months, or the strong names of powerful American businessmen.

At Gatsby's house during the summer, I remember several other people being there. Faustina O'Brien came at least once, as did the Baedeker girls and young Brewer, who'd lost his nose in the war. Mr. Albrucksburger and his fiancée, Miss Haag, were also in attendance, along with Ardita Fitz-Peters and Mr. P. Jewett, a former leader of the American Legion. Miss Claudia Hip arrived with a man who we assumed was her chauffeur, as well as a prince who we nicknamed Duke, whose actual name, if I ever knew it, has slipped my mind.

All of these individuals came to Gatsby's house during the summer.

~

ONE MORNING IN LATE JULY, at nine o'clock, Gatsby's magnificent car veered up the uneven driveway to my door, emitting a burst of melody from its distinctive three-toned horn.

This was the first time he had extended an invitation to me, despite my attending two of his parties and riding in his hydroplane, as well as frequently using his beach at his insistence.

"Good morning, old sport. You're joining me for lunch today, and I thought we could ride together," he said.

He balanced himself on the car's dashboard with a certain American resourcefulness of movement, a quality that arises, I suppose, from the lack of physically demanding work during youth and, even more so, from the fluid grace of our sporadic, high-energy games. This characteristic continually broke through his polished manner in the form of restlessness. He was never quite still; there was always a foot tapping somewhere or his hands restlessly opening and closing.

He noticed me admiring his car.

"It's quite lovely, don't you think?" He hopped off to give me a better view. "Have you seen it before?"

I had seen it. Everyone had seen it. The car was a rich cream color, gleaming with nickel accents. The windshields formed a complex maze that reflected the sunlight. We settled into the plush green leather seats, surrounded by layers of glass, and began our journey to town.

Over the past month, I had spoken with him a handful of times and discovered that he had very little to say. My initial impression of him as someone of some importance had gradually faded. He had become simply the owner of a lavish roadside establishment next door.

And then came that bewildering ride. He was talking eloquently. But soon, he nervously slapped his knee, unsure of himself in his caramel-colored suit.

"Listen carefully, old sport," he burst out unexpectedly. "What do you honestly think of me?"

Feeling slightly overwhelmed, I began offering vague responses.

"Well, let me tell you a bit about my life," he interjected. "I don't want you to form any opinions about me based on the stories you hear."

So he was aware of the strange rumors that circulated among his guests.

"I'll tell you the honest truth." He raised his right hand dramatically. "I come from a wealthy family in the Midwest, but they're all gone now. I grew up in America but got my education at Oxford. It's a family tradition."

He glanced at me sideways. I understood why Jordan Baker

thought he was lying. He rushed through the phrase "educated at Oxford," as if was hard to say. Doubts started to creep in.

"Which part of the Midwest?" I asked casually.

"San Francisco. All my family died, and I inherited a lot of money."

His voice turned sad, as if the memory of his family's sudden demise still haunted him. Part of me thought he might be joking, but a quick look at him changed my mind.

"After that, I lived like a wealthy prince in European capitals like Paris, Venice, and Rome. I collected jewels, mostly rubies, went on big game hunts, dabbled in painting for my own pleasure, and tried to forget something very sad that happened to me a long time ago."

I struggled to hold back my laughter at his exaggerated claims. The phrases he used sounded made him sound as though he was delivering a fairy tale.

"Then the war came, my friend. It was a huge relief, and I tried my best to die. But it seemed like I had an enchanted life. I joined as a first lieutenant when the war started. In the Argonne Forest, I led my machine-gun battalion so far ahead that there was a gap of half a mile on each side where the infantry couldn't move forward. We stayed there for two days and two nights, with a hundred and thirty men and sixteen Lewis guns. When the infantry finally arrived, they found the insignia of three German divisions among the piles of dead. I was promoted to major, and I received decorations from every Allied government, even Montenegro, a small country along the Adriatic Sea!"

He emphasized the words "Little Montenegro" and nodded, flashing a smile. The smile expressed an understanding of Montenegro's troubled history and the courageous struggles of its people. He acknowledged the series of events that led to this tribute from Montenegro's passionate heart. My doubt was now overshadowed by fascination. It felt like quickly flipping through a dozen magazines.

He reached into his pocket, and a piece of metal on a ribbon fell into my hand.

"That's the one from Montenegro."

To my surprise, it looked authentic. The circular engraving read, "Orderi di Danilo, Montenegro, Nicolas Rex."

"Turn it around."

"Major Jay Gatsby," I read, "For Exceptional Courage."

"Here's something else I always carry, a memento from my days at Oxford. It's a photograph taken in Trinity Quad—the person on my left is now the Earl of Doncaster."

The photograph showed a group of young men in blazers relaxing in an archway, with multiple towering spires in the background. Gatsby was among them, appearing slightly younger and holding a cricket bat.

As I looked at the photo, I couldn't help but believe it was all true. I was better able to imagine him inside his stories.

"Today, I'm going to make a big request of you," he said, pleased with his souvenirs as he tucked them away. "So, I thought you should know a bit about me. I didn't want you to think I was just some unknown person. You see, I often find myself among strangers because I wander here and there, trying to forget the sad events that have occurred in my life." He paused. "You'll hear about it this afternoon."

"During lunch?" I asked.

"No, this afternoon. I happened to discover that you are taking Miss Baker for tea."

"Are you saying you're in love with Miss Baker?"

"No, my friend, I'm not. But Miss Baker has kindly agreed to discuss this matter with you."

I had no clue what "this matter" was, but I felt more annoyed than curious. I hadn't invited Jordan for tea to discuss Mr. Jay Gatsby. I was certain the request would be something completely absurd. For a moment, I regretted ever stepping onto his overcrowded lawn.

80　He wouldn't speak anymore. He became even more proper as we approached the city. We passed Port Roosevelt, where we caught a glimpse the ships. Then, on both sides of us, the desolate area known as the valley of ashes came into view, and I saw Mrs. Wilson pumping gas at a garage with excited energy as we drove by.

We drove a little further and I heard the familiar sound of a motorcycle's engine and saw a frantic policeman riding alongside us.

"All right, old sport," Gatsby called out. We slowed down. He took out a white card from his wallet and waved it in front of the police officer's eyes.

"That's right," the policeman agreed, tipping his cap. "I'll recognize you next time, Mr. Gatsby. Sorry for the hassle!"

"What was that about?" I asked. "Did you show him a picture of Oxford?"

"I did a favor for the police commissioner once, and now he sends me a Christmas card every year."

We crossed the great bridge. The view of the city from the Queensboro Bridge always feels like the first time you've ever seen it, with all its wonder and beauty still unexplored.

81　A dead man rode by in a vehicle filled with flowers, followed by two carriages with closed blinds and more carriages for mourners. The mourners, who had sad eyes and stoic expressions, were from southeastern Europe. It made me happy that they could see Gatsby's impressive car during their somber occasion. As we crossed Blackwell's Island, a limousine driven by a white chauffeur passed us. Inside were three fashionable African Americans.

"Now that we've crossed this bridge," I thought, "anything is possible...even Gatsby, without any sense of amazement."

~

IT WAS a bustling noon when I met Gatsby for lunch in a cool underground space on Forty-second Street. My eyes adjusted to the dimness after being blinded by the brightness outside. I spotted Gatsby talking to another man in the anteroom.

"Mr. Carraway, this is my friend Mr. Wolfshiem," Gatsby introduced.

A small Jewish man raised his head and looked at me. He had luxurious hair growing from both nostrils.

"So, I took one look at him," Mr. Wolfshiem said, shaking my hand with enthusiasm, "and guess what I did?"

"What?" I asked politely.

But it seemed like he wasn't addressing me just then. He let go of my hand and focused his attention on Gatsby, inspecting him closely with his distinctive nose.

"I handed the money to Katspaugh and I said: 'Alright, Katspaugh, don't pay him a penny until he stops talking.' He stopped right then and there."

Gatsby took an arm of each of us and led us into the restaurant, causing Mr. Wolfshiem to abandon the sentence he was about to utter and drift into a daydream.

"Drinks?" asked the head waiter.

"This is a nice restaurant," Mr. Wolfshiem remarked, looking up at the pictures on the ceiling. "But I prefer the one across the street!"

"Yes, drinks," Gatsby agreed, and then to Mr. Wolfshiem: "It's too hot over there."

"Hot and small—yes," Mr. Wolfshiem replied. "But full of memories."

"What place is that?" I asked.

"The old Metropole."

"The old Metropole," Mr. Wolfshiem mused with sadness. "Filled with faces from the past. Filled with friends now gone forever. I can't forget the night they shot Rosy Rosenthal there as long as I live. There were six of us at the table, and Rosy had been eating and drinking heavily all night. When it was almost morning, the waiter approached him with a peculiar expression and said someone wanted to talk to him outside. 'Alright,' said Rosy, starting to get up, and I pulled him back into his seat.

" 'Let those bastards come in here if they want you, Rosy. But I swear to you, don't you move outside this room.'

"It was four o'clock in the morning then, and if we had lifted the blinds, we would have seen daylight."

"Did he go?" I innocently asked.

"Of course he went," Mr. Wolfshiem responded with anger in his voice. "He turned around at the door and said, 'Don't let that waiter take away my coffee!' Then he went outside on the sidewalk, and they shot him three times in his stomach and drove away."

"Four of them were executed," I said, remembering it now.

"Five, including Becker," Mr. Wolfshiem informed eagerly. "I heard you were looking for a business connection."

The sudden change in topic was surprising. Gatsby intervened, speaking on my behalf:

"Oh, no," he exclaimed, "this is not the man."

"No?" Mr. Wolfshiem appeared disappointed.

"This is just a friend. I told you we would discuss that another time."

"I apologize," said Mr. Wolfshiem, "I had the wrong person."

A delicious dish arrived, and Mr. Wolfshiem began to eat. His eyes wandered slowly around the room, occasionally pausing to observe the people sitting directly behind us. I believe that if I were not present, he would have taken a quick glance under our table.

"Listen here, my friend," Gatsby said, leaning towards me, "I'm afraid I made you a little upset this morning in the car."

The smile reappeared, but this time I resisted it.

"I don't like secrets," I replied, "and I don't understand why you can't be direct and tell me what you want. Why does everything have to involve Miss Baker?"

"Oh, it's nothing sneaky," he reassured me. "Miss Baker is a great athlete, you know, and she would never do anything that wasn't okay."

Suddenly, he checked his watch, got up, and hurried out of the room, leaving me with Mr. Wolfshiem at the table.

"He has to make a phone call," said Mr. Wolfshiem, watching him go. "Impressive guy, isn't he? Handsome and a true gentleman."

"Yes."

"He attended Oggsford College."

"Oh!"

"He went to Oggsford College in England. Have you heard of it?"

"I've heard of it."

"It's one of the most famous colleges in the world."

"How long have you known Gatsby?" I asked.

"For several years," he answered proudly. "I had the pleasure of meeting him shortly after the war. And after talking to him for just an hour, I knew he was a man of exceptional upbringing. I thought to myself, 'There's the kind of man you'd want to bring home and introduce to your mother and sister.'" He paused. "I notice you're looking at my cufflinks."

I hadn't been, but I examined them now. They were made of oddly familiar pieces of ivory.

"They're the finest human molar specimens," he informed me.

"Well!" I inspected them. "That's a very interesting idea."

"Yeah." He rolled up his sleeves under his coat. "Yeah, Gatsby is very respectful towards women. He would never even look at a friend's wife."

When Gatsby returned to the table and sat down, Mr. Wolfshiem quickly finished his coffee and stood up.

"I enjoyed my lunch," he said, "and I'm going to leave before I overstay my welcome."

"No need to rush, Meyer," said Gatsby unenthused. Mr. Wolfshiem raised his hand in a blessing-like gesture.

"You're very polite, but I come from a different generation," he declared solemnly. "You young men can sit here and discuss your sports and your young ladies and your..." He gestured with his hand to fill in the blank. "As for me, I'm fifty years old, and I won't impose on you any longer."

As he shook hands and walked away, his sad expression trembled. I wondered if I had said something to upset him.

"He's prone to sentimentality at times," Gatsby explained. "Today is one of those days. He's quite a character in New York—a regular on Broadway."

"Who is he, anyway, an actor?"

"No."

"A dentist?"

"Meyer Wolfshiem? No, he's a gambler." Gatsby paused, then added casually, "He's the man who rigged the outcome of the World's Series in 1919."

"He rigged the World's Series?" I repeated.

The idea stunned me. I remembered, of course, that the World's Series had been fixed in 1919. It never occurred to me that one man could toy with the trust of fifty million people, with the focused determination of a thief cracking a safe.

"How did he end up doing that?" I asked after a moment.

"He saw the opportunity and took it, just like that."

"Why isn't he in jail?" I asked.

"They can't catch him, old buddy. He's pretty clever," replied Gatsby.

I insisted on paying the bill, and as the waiter handed me my change, I noticed Tom Buchanan across the crowded room.

"Come with me for a moment, I need to greet someone," I said.

Tom jumped up when he saw us and quickly walked over to us.

"Where have you been?" he asked eagerly. "Daisy is furious because you haven't called."

"This is Mr. Gatsby, Mr. Buchanan," I introduced them.

They shook hands briefly, and Gatsby's face showed a tense, awkward expression.

"How have you been, by the way?" Tom asked me. "Why did you come all the way here to have lunch?"

"I had lunch with Mr. Gatsby," I replied.

As I turned to look at him, Gatsby had already disappeared from sight.

~

ON AN OCTOBER DAY IN 1917—

(Jordan Baker said that afternoon, sitting upright in a chair at the tea-garden in the Plaza Hotel)

—I was walking from one place to another, partly on the side-walks and partly on the lawns. I preferred walking on the lawns as I had shoes from England with rubber knobs on the soles, which helped me grip the soft ground. I was also wearing a new plaid skirt that gently fluttered in the wind. Whenever this happened, the red, white, and blue banners in front of the houses stood straight as if scolding, saying tut-tut-tut-tut, disapprovingly.

The biggest of the banners and the largest of the lawns belonged to Daisy Fay's house. She was only eighteen, two years older than me, and the most popular among all the young girls in Louisville. She always wore white and had a small white convertible. All day long, the telephone in her house would ring with calls from excited young officers from Camp Taylor, all hoping to spend the evening exclu-sively with her. "At least for an hour!"

That morning, as I walked past her house, her white convertible was parked by the curb. She was sitting inside with a lieutenant whom I had never seen before. They were so absorbed in each other that she didn't notice me until I was just five feet away.

"Hey, Jordan!" she called out unexpectedly. "Please come over here."

I felt flattered that she wanted to talk to me, as I admired her the most among all the older girls. She asked if I was heading to the Red Cross to make bandages. I was. Well, then, could I let them know that she couldn't come that day? I noticed how the officer looked at Daisy while she spoke, in a way that every young girl wishes to be looked at at some point. This romantic moment stuck with me. His name was Jay Gatsby, and I didn't see him again for over four years—even when I met him on Long Island, it didn't occur to me that he was the same man.

That happened in 1917. The following year, I started dating a few guys myself and began playing in tournaments, so I didn't see Daisy very often. She hung out with an older crowd, if she hung out with anyone at all. There were rumors going around about her. People said her mother caught her trying to pack her bags one night to go to New York and say goodbye to a soldier who was going overseas. Her mother managed to stop her, but they didn't speak to each other for weeks. After that, she stopped fooling around with soldiers and only spent time with a few average guys in town who were unfit for the military.

By the next fall, she was happy again, just as happy as she had been before. She made her debut after the armistice, and in February, she was supposedly engaged to a man from New Orleans. In June, she married Tom Buchanan from Chicago with more grandeur and celebration than Louisville had ever known. He arrived with a hundred people in four private train cars and booked an entire floor of the Muhlbach Hotel. The day before the wedding, he gave her a string of pearls worth three hundred and fifty thousand dollars.

I was one of the bridesmaids. I entered her room half an hour before the rehearsal dinner and found her lying on her bed, looking as beautiful as the June night in her floral dress—and completely drunk. She had a bottle of Sauterne in one hand and a letter in the other.

"Congratulate me," she slurred. "I've never had a drink before, but oh, how I enjoy it."

"What's wrong, Daisy?" I felt a wave of fear wash over me; I had never seen a girl in such a state as this before.

With a wastebasket by her side on the bed, she fumbled through it and retrieved a string of pearls. "Take these downstairs, darlings, and return them to their rightful owner. Inform them that Daisy has changed her mind. Say: 'Daisy has changed her mind!'"

Tears streamed down her face; she sobbed uncontrollably. I hurriedly left the room and sought out her mother's maid. Together, we locked the door and managed to get Daisy into a cold bath. Despite her resistance, she clutched onto the letter tightly. She brought it with her into the tub and crumpled it into a sodden ball. Reluctantly, she allowed me to place it in the soap dish, only when she realized it was disintegrating like snow.

However, she didn't utter another word. Administering spirits of ammonia and applying ice to her forehead, we managed to get her dressed again. Half an hour later, when we left the room, the pearls adorned her neck and the incident was behind us. The next day, at five o'clock, she married Tom Buchanan without a hint of hesitation and embarked on a three-month journey to the South Seas.

90   I saw them in Santa Barbara when they returned, and I thought I had never seen a girl so infatuated with her husband. If he left the room for even a moment, she would grow restless and ask, "Where's Tom?" and wear a distracted expression until she spotted him entering the door. They would sit on the beach for hours, with her caressing his face and gazing at him with indescribable joy. It was endearing to witness their togetherness--it evoked both laughter and fascination. This happened in August. A week after I left Santa Barbara, Tom had an accident on the Ventura road, colliding with a wagon which caused one of his car's front wheels to rip off. The girl who was with him also made it into the news, as she had broken her arm--she worked as one of the chambermaids at the Santa Barbara Hotel.

The following April, Daisy gave birth to their daughter, and they spent a year in France. I encountered them one spring in Cannes, and later in Deauville, before they eventually returned to settle in Chicago. Daisy was well-liked in Chicago, as you may know. They kept company with a lively crowd, consisting of young, wealthy, and reckless individuals, yet Daisy managed to maintain a pristine reputation. Perhaps her abstinence from alcohol played a part. It's an advantage not to drink when surrounded by heavy drinkers. It enables one to stay silent and, furthermore, to time any personal lapses in such a way that others are too oblivious or uninterested to notice. Maybe Daisy never indulged in affairs at all, and yet, there's something captivating about her voice...

A few weeks ago, she heard the name Gatsby for the first time in years. It happened when I asked you if you knew Gatsby in West Egg. Later, when you had left, she came into my room and woke me up. She asked, "Who is this Gatsby?" As I described him, half-asleep, she said in a strange voice that he must be the man she used to know. It was then that I made the connection between Gatsby and the officer in her white car.

After Jordan Baker finished telling me all of this, we left the Plaza and began driving in a horse-drawn carriage through Central Park. The sun had set behind the tall apartment buildings where the movie stars lived. In the warm twilight, the clear voices of children, gathered on the grass like crickets, filled the air:

"I'm the Sheik of Araby,

Your love belongs to me.

At night when you're asleep,

Into your tent, I'll creep--"

"It was a strange coincidence," I said.

"But it wasn't a coincidence at all."

"Why not?"

"Gatsby bought that house so that Daisy would be just across the bay."

In that moment, I realized that Gatsby's ambitions on that June night went beyond reaching for the stars. He became alive to me, suddenly freed from his empty and extravagant lifestyle.

"He wants to know," Jordan continued, "if you would invite Daisy to your house one afternoon and then allow him to come over."

The simplicity of his request surprised me. He had waited for five years and bought a grand house, where he glowed like a star, attracting curious onlookers. And all he wanted was to "come over" to a stranger's garden one afternoon.

"Did I need to know all of this before he could ask for such a small favor?"

"He's scared, he's waited so long. He thought you might be upset. You see, deep down, he's actually quite tough."

Something concerned me.

"Why didn't he ask you to arrange a meeting?"

"He wants her to see his house," she explained. "And your house is right next to his."

"Oh!"

"I think he half expected her to stumble into one of his parties one night," Jordan continued, "but she never did. So, he started casually asking people if they knew her, and I happened to be the first one he found. That night, he summoned me during his dance, and you should have heard the elaborate way he built up to it. Of course, I immediately suggested a lunch in New York—and I thought he would go crazy:

'I don't want to do anything unusual!' he kept saying. 'I just want to see her right next door.'

"When I mentioned that you were a close friend of Tom's, he almost gave up on the whole idea. He doesn't know much about Tom, even though he claims to have read a Chicago newspaper for years, just in the hope of catching a glimpse of Daisy's name."

It was getting dark now, and as we went under a small bridge, I put my arm around Jordan's golden shoulder and pulled her closer to me, asking her to join me for dinner. Suddenly, I wasn't thinking about Daisy and Gatsby anymore. Instead, I was focused on this straightforward, tough, but limited person next to me. She had a way of leaning back confidently within the circle of my arm. A phrase echoed in my mind with a thrilling excitement: "There are only those who are chased, those who chase, those who are busy, and those who are tired."

"And Daisy deserves to have something in her life," Jordan whispered to me.

"Does she want to see Gatsby?"

"She can't know about it. Gatsby doesn't want her to know. You're only supposed to invite her for tea."

We passed through a dark area of trees and then entered the elegant glow of Fifty-Ninth Street, where delicate lights from the buildings illuminated the park. Unlike Gatsby and Tom Buchanan, I didn't have a girl whose ethereal face appeared in my mind along with the shadows and blinding signs. So, I brought the girl closer to me, holding her tightly. She smiled with a hint of contempt on her pale lips, so I drew her even closer, this time towards my face.

CHAPTER

FIVE

 WHEN I ARRIVED home in West Egg that night, I briefly panicked, fearing that my house was on fire. I realized that it was Gatsby's house, brilliantly lit from top to bottom.

Initially, I believed it to be another extravagant party, a lively gathering with the entire house open for the participants. However, there was no sound, only the rustling of the wind in the trees. As my taxi departed with a groan, I spotted Gatsby walking towards me across his lawn.

"Your place looks like the World's Fair," I remarked.

"Does it?" He turned his eyes towards his house. "I've been glancing into some of the rooms. Let's go to Coney Island, old friend, in my car."

"It's too late."

"Well, what if we take a dip in the swimming pool? I haven't used it all summer."

"I need to go to bed. Oh, I spoke with Miss Baker," I continued after a moment. "I'm planning to call Daisy tomorrow and invite her for tea."

"Oh, that's alright," he replied. "I don't want to inconvenience you."

"Which day would be best for you?"

"What day works for you?" he asked quickly, correcting my wording. "I don't want to inconvenience you, you know."

"How about the day after tomorrow?"

He pondered for a moment. Then, with some reluctance, he replied, "I need to mow the lawn."

We both glanced down at the grass—there was a noticeable line where my unkempt lawn met the darker, well-maintained area of his. I suspected he was referring to my lawn.

"There's another small matter," he said uncertainly, hesitating.

"Would you rather postpone it for a few days?" I suggested.

"Oh, it's not about that. Well—" He struggled with his words. "I had this thought—listen, old friend, you don't make much money, do you?"

"Not very much."

This seemed to put him at ease, and he continued more confidently.

"I figured as much. If you don't mind, I have a little side business, a sort of secondary venture, you see. And I thought that since you don't earn much—You're selling bonds, right, old sport?"

"Trying to."

"Well, this might interest you. It wouldn't require much of your time, and you could earn a decent sum of money. It happens to be rather confidential."

Looking back, I now realize that under different circumstances, that conversation could have been a turning point in my life. However, I had to go.

"I'm really busy right now," I replied. "I appreciate the offer, but I can't take on any more work."

"Oh, you wouldn't have to do any business with Wolfshiem," he said. It seemed like he thought I was avoiding the connection that was mentioned at lunch. He waited for a moment, hoping for a conversation, but we ended it there.

The evening had left me feeling light and happy. I believe I fell into a deep sleep as soon as I stepped inside my house. The next morning, I called Daisy from the office and invited her to come over for tea.

"Just make sure not to bring Tom," I warned her.

"What?" she asked innocently.

"Don't bring Tom."

"Who is 'Tom'?" she asked, playing along.

It was pouring rain on the day we agreed to meet. At eleven o'clock, a man in a raincoat, dragging a lawn-mower, knocked on my front door and informed me that Mr. Gatsby had sent him to mow my grass. This reminded me that I had forgotten to ask my Finnish woman to come back, so I drove to West Egg Village to search for her among wet, whitewashed streets and to purchase some cups, lemons, and flowers.

At two o'clock, an entire greenhouse arrived from Gatsby's house with numerous plant holders. An hour later, Gatsby entered nervously through the front door. He was wearing a white suit, a silver shirt, and a gold-colored tie, but he looked pale and had dark circles under his eyes.

"Is everything okay?" he immediately asked.

"If you're talking about the grass, it looks fine."

"What grass?" he asked with a puzzled expression. "Oh, you mean the grass in the yard." He rambled a bit, "One of the newspapers said the rain might stop around four. I think it was The Journal. Do you have everything you need for tea?"

I led him into the pantry, where he gave a slightly disapproving look at the Finn. We both examined the twelve lemon cakes I'd bought from the deli.

"Are these good enough?" I asked.

"Of course, of course! They're fine!" he replied with a hollow tone, "... old sport."

The rain stopped around three-thirty and turned into a mist, with occasional light drops falling like dew. Every now and then, he glanced towards the blurry windows as if something invisible and worrisome was happening outside. Eventually, he stood up and said uncertainly that he was going home.

"Why?" I asked.

"No one is coming for tea. It's too late!" He checked his watch as if he had some urgent appointment elsewhere. "I can't wait all day."

"Don't be silly. She'll be here in a few minutes."

He sat down miserably, as if I had pushed him, and at that moment, we heard the sound of a car turning into my driveway. Startled, both of us stood up, and feeling a bit unsettled myself, I walked out into the yard.

A large open car stopped under the dripping lilac trees. Daisy's face, tilted sideways under a lavender hat with three corners, looked out at me with a bright, ecstatic smile.

"Is this absolutely where you live, my dear?"

The sound of her voice was like a burst of energy in the rain. I had to listen closely with just my ear for a moment before I could make out the words. I took her hand and helped her from the car.

"Are you in love with me?" she whispered quietly in my ear. "Or else, why did I have to come alone?"

"That's the mystery of Castle Rackrent. Tell your chauffeur to go far away and give us an hour."

"Come back in an hour, Ferdie." Then, in a serious tone, she added, "His name is Ferdie."

"Does the smell of gasoline bother him?"

"I don't think so," she replied innocently. "Why?"

We entered the house. To my great surprise, the living room was empty.

"Well, that's odd," I exclaimed.

"What's odd?" she asked, turning her head just as there was a polite knock at the front door. I went to open it. Gatsby, pale as a ghost, with his hands buried deep in his coat pockets, stood in a puddle of water, glaring tragically into my eyes.

Without taking his hands out of his pockets, he walked past me and disappeared into the living room. It was not funny at all. As the rain grew heavier, I closed the door, aware of the pounding of my own heart.

For what felt like an eternity, there was silence. Then, from the living room, I heard a muffled murmur and a fragment of laughter, followed by Daisy's voice, sounding insincere and forced:

"I'm certainly very glad to see you again."

There was a pause, an uncomfortably long pause. With nothing else to do in the hallway, I decided to enter the room.

Gatsby, with his hands still in his pockets, was leaning against the fireplace mantel in a forced attempt to appear relaxed. He nearly tipped over the old mantel clock as he looked at Daisy, who was sitting nervously but gracefully.

"We've met before," whispered Gatsby. His eyes briefly glanced at me, and his lips made a failed attempt at a laugh. He almost knocked over a clock, but caught it.

My face was burning. "It's an old clock," I foolishly commented.

Then Gatsby and Daisy realized it had been five years since they'd seen one another.

In an attempt to break the tension, I suggested that we make tea in the kitchen. Then the housekeeper brought it in on a tray.

In the midst of the enjoyable chaos of cups and treats, a sense of respectability settled. Gatsby positioned himself in the shadows, observing both Daisy and me with anxious eyes. However, since tranquility was not the main goal, I quickly made an excuse and stood up.

"Where are you going?" Gatsby asked, alarmed.

"I'll be back."

"I need to talk to you about something before you leave. This is a terrible mistake," he said, shaking his head sadly. "A terrible, terrible mistake."

"You're just embarrassed, that's all," I reassured him. "And, luckily, Daisy is embarrassed too. You're acting childish," I said. "Don't leave her sitting there alone."

He raised his hand to me. He was annoyed, but he went back in.

102   I walked out the back way, just like Gatsby had done earlier, as he anxiously circled the house. I hurried towards a large dark tangled tree, where the thick leaves provided a shelter from the rain. It was pouring again, and Gatsby's well-maintained lawn, carefully trimmed by his gardener, was filled with small muddy patches and ancient swamps. There was nothing else to see besides Gatsby's immense house, so I gazed at it, much like Kant gazing at a church steeple, for about thirty minutes. The house had been built by a brewer during the trend of that time, a decade ago, and there was a tale that the brewer had agreed to pay five years' worth of taxes for all the nearby cottages if the owners would thatch their roofs with straw. Maybe their refusal had crushed his dreams of starting a family, and he quickly fell into a decline. His children eventually sold the house with the black wreath still hanging on the door. Americans, who were willing and even eager to be servants, have always been stubborn about being treated as peasants.

103   After thirty minutes, the sun came out again, and the grocer's car drove up Gatsby's driveway with the ingredients for his servants' dinner. I was certain he wouldn't eat a bite. A maid started to open the windows on the upper floor of his house, appearing briefly in each one. From the large central bay window, she leaned out and spat thoughtfully into the garden. It was time for me to return. While it was still raining, it seemed like I could hear the faint murmur of voices from inside, occasionally rising and swelling with bursts of emotion. But in the newfound silence, I sensed that an aura of silence had also descended upon the house.

I entered, purposely making as much noise as possible in the kitchen without actually knocking over the stove. I don't think they heard a single sound. They were sitting on opposite ends of the couch, their gaze locked as if some question had been asked, or was hanging in the air, and any trace of awkwardness had vanished. Daisy's face was streaked with tears, and when I walked in, she quickly stood up and began wiping them away with her handkerchief in front of a mirror. But the change in Gatsby was perplexing. He seemed to emit a literal glow; there was no need for words or triumphant gestures, as a newfound sense of well-being radiated from him and filled the small room.

"Oh, hello there, old friend," he said, as if we hadn't seen each other in years. For a moment, I thought he might reach out to shake hands.

"The rain has stopped."

"Has it?" When he realized what I meant, that there were glimpses of sunlight in the room, he smiled like a weatherman, full of joy for the return of light, and shared the news with Daisy. "Can you believe it? The rain has finally stopped."

"I'm so glad, Jay." Her voice, filled with both grief and happiness, expressed her unexpected joy.

"I want both you and Daisy to come to my house," he said. "I'd like to give her a tour."

"Are you sure you want me to come?"

"Absolutely, my friend."

Daisy went upstairs to freshen up--I couldn't help but feel embarrassed about my humble towels. Meanwhile, Gatsby and I waited on the lawn.

"Doesn't my house look impressive?" he asked. "Look how the front of it catches the light."

I agreed that it looked magnificent.

"Yes." His gaze swept over every detail--the arched doors, the square towers. "It took me only three years to earn the money that bought this place."

"I thought you inherited your wealth."

"I did, my friend," he said automatically, "but I lost most of it during the war's financial crisis."

I believe he hardly knew what he was saying, because when I

inquired about his line of work, he replied, "That's my personal matter," before realizing it was not an appropriate response.

"Oh, I have been involved in various ventures," he corrected himself. "I used to work in pharmaceuticals, then I shifted to the oil industry. But I am not involved in either of them anymore." He looked at me more intently. "Does that mean you have been considering my proposal from the other night?"

Daisy came out of the house. The buttons on her dress sparkled in the sun.

"That enormous place over there?" she exclaimed, pointing.

"Do you like it?"

"I love it, but I don't understand how you can live there all alone."

"I always keep it filled with interesting people, day and night. People who do fascinating things. Famous people."

Instead of taking the shorter way along the Sound, we walked down to the road and entered through the large entrance. Daisy was in awe of the flowers, marble steps, and birds flying around. We did not see any people though.

We wandered through Gatsby's palace in silence. I wondered if Owl Eyes was still in the library.

We went upstairs, passing through historical bedrooms decorated with soft pink and purple silk and vibrant fresh flowers. We moved through dressing rooms, game rooms, and bathrooms with sunken tubs. In one of the rooms, we intruded upon a disheveled man in pajamas doing floor exercises. It was Mr. Klipspringer, the "tenant." I had seen him wandering eagerly on the beach earlier that morning. Eventually, we arrived at Gatsby's own living quarters, which consisted of a bedroom, a bathroom, and a study with antique furniture. There, we sat down and enjoyed a glass of Chartreuse that Gatsby took from a hidden cupboard in the wall.

Gatsby never took his eyes off Daisy, as if he was reassessing everything in his house based on her reaction. At times, he glanced around at his belongings with a bewildered expression, as if they no longer seemed real in her presence. He even came close to falling down a flight of stairs.

His bedroom was the most simple room of all, with the exception of a dresser adorned with a dull gold vanity set. Daisy happily picked up the brush and gently smoothed her hair, causing Gatsby to sit down, cover his eyes, and burst into laughter.

"It's the most amusing thing, old sport," he said, filled with hilarity. "I can't—whenever I try to—"

He had gone through two distinct emotions and now he was experiencing a new one. After feeling embarrassed and then overwhelmingly happy, he was now filled with awe at the sight of her. He had held onto the idea for so long, imagining it in great detail, and waited anxiously for this moment. But now, as the excitement waned, he felt like an over-wound clock starting to slow down.

After collecting himself, he opened two large cabinets that contained his collection of suits, dressing gowns, ties, and shirts. The shirts were stacked high, like bricks in a strong structure.

"I have a man in England who buys my clothes. He sends me a selection of items at the beginning of each season, in spring and fall."

He pulled out a stack of shirts and started tossing them one by one in front of us. The shirts, made of thin linen, thick silk, and fine flannel, lost their creases as they fell and created a colorful mess on the table. As we admired the shirts, he brought even more, piling them up higher and higher. The shirts had stripes, patterns, and plaid designs in vibrant shades of coral, apple-green, lavender, and pale orange. Some even had monograms in dark blue. Suddenly, Daisy leaned into the shirts and began crying loudly.

"These shirts are so beautiful," she sobbed, her voice muffled by the thick fabric. "It makes me sad because I've never seen such lovely shirts before."

～

AFTER WE TOURED THE HOUSE, we were supposed to explore the grounds, the swimming pool, and the hydroplane, as well as admire the summer flowers. However, it started raining again outside Gatsby's window, so we gathered in a line and stared at the wavy surface of the Sound.

"If the mist wasn't here, we could see your house across the bay," Gatsby remarked. "You always have a green light that glows all night at the end of your dock."

Daisy quickly linked her arm through his, but he seemed lost in his own thoughts. Maybe he had realized that the immense importance of that light had now disappeared forever. It had seemed so close to Daisy, almost within reach, compared to the great distance that had separated him from her. It appeared as near as a star to the moon. Now it was just a green light on a dock. The number of magical things in his world had decreased by one.

I began to wander around the room, examining various vague objects in the dim light. One particular object caught my attention— a large photograph of an older man dressed in a yachting outfit, hanging on the wall above his desk.

"Who's this?" I asked.

"Oh, that? That's Mr. Dan Cody, old buddy."

The name sounded vaguely familiar.

"He's passed away now. He used to be my closest friend many years ago."

There was a small picture of Gatsby on the dresser, also in a yachting costume, with his head defiantly thrown back. It seemed to be taken when he was around eighteen.

"I love it!" Daisy exclaimed. "The pompadour! You never mentioned you had a pompadour—or a yacht."

"Take a look at this," Gatsby said quickly. "Here are a bunch of newspaper clippings about you."

They stood next to each other, examining the clippings. I was about to ask to see the rubies when the phone rang, and Gatsby picked it up.

"Yes... Well, I can't talk right now... I can't talk now, old friend... I said a small town... He should know what a small town is... Well, he's useless to us if he thinks Detroit is a small town..."

He hung up.

"Come here quickly!" Daisy exclaimed from the window.

The rain was still falling, but the sky was clearing in the west, revealing a beautiful display of pink and golden clouds above the sea.

"Look at that," she whispered, and then after a moment: "I wish I could just take one of those pink clouds and put you inside it, and push you around."

I tried to leave then, but they insisted I stay; perhaps my presence made them feel more comfortably alone.

"I know what we'll do," Gatsby said. "We'll have Klipspringer play the piano."

He left the room calling out, "Ewing!" and returned a few minutes later with an embarrassed, slightly tired young man. The man had glasses with shell-shaped frames and thin blond hair. He was now dressed decently in a casual shirt, open at the collar, sneakers, and light-colored pants.

"Did we interrupt your workout?" Daisy asked politely.

"I was sleeping," Mr. Klipspringer blurted out, clearly embarrassed. "Well, I had been sleeping. Then I got up..."

"Klipspringer plays the piano," Gatsby said, cutting him off. "Isn't that right, Ewing, old friend?"

"I'm not very good at playing the piano. I hardly play at all. I haven't practiced—"

"We can go downstairs," Gatsby interrupted. He flipped a switch, and the grey windows disappeared as the house filled with light.

In the music room, Gatsby turned on a lamp next to the piano. He used a trembling match to light Daisy's cigarette, then sat with her on a couch across the room, where they sat in dim light that bounced in from the hall.

After Klipspringer played "The Love Nest," he turned around on the bench and searched for Gatsby in the dark.

"I haven't practiced much, you see. I told you I couldn't play. I haven't practiced—"

"Don't talk so much, old sport," Gatsby commanded. "Play!"

"In the morning, in the evening, ain't we got fun—"

Outside, the wind was loud and there was a faint sound of thunder along the Sound. All the lights in West Egg were turning on now. Electric trains carrying people were rushing home through the rain from New York. It was a time of great change, and excitement filled the air.

"One thing's sure and nothing's surer. The rich get richer and the poor get—children. In the meantime, in between time—"

As I walked over to say goodbye, I noticed the perplexed expression returning to Gatsby's face. It seemed as though he had a faint doubt about the true extent of his current happiness. Almost five years had passed! There must have been moments that afternoon when Daisy fell short of his lofty dreams. This was not her fault, but rather a result of the overwhelming power of his own illusion. It had grown beyond her, beyond everything. He had immersed himself in it with an intense passion, constantly enhancing it with every opportunity that came his way. No amount of passion or freshness could challenge what a man can hold in his deep, hidden heart.

As I watched him, I could see him adjusting himself slightly, clear as day. He reached out and took her hand, and as she whispered something softly into his ear, he turned towards her with a rush of emotion. I believe it was her voice that captivated him the most, with its fluctuating, feverish warmth. It was a voice that couldn't be over-imagined; it was a timeless melody.

They had forgotten about my presence, but Daisy looked up and extended her hand towards me. Gatsby didn't recognize me anymore. I glanced at them one last time, and they glanced back at me, distantly, captivated by their intense existence. Then, I left the room and descended the marble steps into the rain, leaving them behind together.

CHAPTER
SIX

 AROUND THIS TIME, a young, ambitious reporter from New York showed up one morning at Gatsby's house and asked if he had any comment to make.

"What is this about?" Gatsby asked politely.

"Well... any statement you want to make," the reporter replied.

After a confusing five minutes, it became clear that the man had heard Gatsby's name mentioned in connection to something.

The reporter's instinct was correct. Gatsby's fame, spread by the hundreds of people who had enjoyed his home had made him newsworthy. There were all kinds of wild rumors about him and his house. It's not easy to explain why James Gatz from North Dakota found satisfaction in these fabrications.

 James Gatz, that was his real, or at least legal, name. He changed it when he was seventeen, at the precise moment when his career began. It was then that he'd seen Dan Cody's yacht anchor down on the most treacherous stretch of Lake Superior. In that afternoon, it was James Gatz who'd been strolling along the shore in a torn green shirt and canvas pants. However, it was already Jay Gatsby who borrowed a rowboat, rowed out to the yacht named Tuolomee, and warned Cody that a strong wind might break the boat in half within thirty minutes.

It seemed like he'd had the name prepared for a long time, even back then. His parents were lazy, unsuccessful farmers, and he'd never truly thought of them as his parents. In truth, Jay Gatsby of West Egg, Long Island, emerged from his idealized vision of himself. He was a son of God, in the literal sense, and he felt he had a duty to serve a grand, tacky, and shallow beauty. So he created the exact version of Jay Gatsby that a seventeen-year-old boy would dream up, and he remained loyal to this idea until the end.

For more than a year, he had been working hard along the southern shore of Lake Superior as a clam digger and a salmon fisherman, doing whatever job provided him with food and a place to sleep. The rough days of labor were strengthening his body, making it tough and brown. He had known women from a young age, and because they spoiled him, he'd become arrogant towards them. He looked down on young, inexperienced girls because they lacked knowledge, and he felt disdain towards others because they seemed overly emotional about things that he thought were obvious due to his self-centeredness.

But deep inside, his heart was always in turmoil. Strange, outlandish thoughts plagued him when he laid in bed at night. His mind would create a wild, flashy universe, while the ticking clock and the moonlight soaked his disheveled clothes on the floor. Each night, he added more and more to the vivid scenes in his imagination, until sleep overtook him completely unaware. These fantasies became an escape for his imagination and offered a glimpse into the unreal parts of reality, as if the foundation of the world was as secure as a fairy's delicate wing.

He just knew he would achieve greatness one day, so he decided to attend St. Olaf's College in southern Minnesota. However, after just two weeks, he realized that the college didn't care about his dreams. He took on the job of a janitor to support himself but eventually returned to Lake Superior. He was still searching for a purpose when he saw Dan Cody's yacht anchored nearby that day.

At the time, Cody was fifty years old and had made his fortune in mining. He had been through several mining rushes, from Nevada to Yukon, and he had become incredibly wealthy through Montana copper. Despite his wealth, Cody's mind was starting to become weak, and many women tried to take advantage of him for his money. The scandalous story of how Ella Kaye, a journalist, had manipulated him and convinced him to sail on a yacht was well-known in 1902. For five years, he had been sailing along various shores when he crossed paths with James Gatz in Little Girl Bay. It was as if they'd been destined to meet.

116   Young Gatz saw the yacht as a symbol of all the beauty and excitement in the world. He probably smiled at Cody because he had learned that people liked him when he smiled. Cody asked him some questions, and one question led to Gatz receiving a new name. Cody quickly realized that Gatz was intelligent and highly ambitious. A few days later, Cody took Gatz to Duluth and bought him a blue coat, six pairs of white trousers, and a yachting cap. When the yacht, Tuolomee, set sail for the West Indies and the Barbary Coast, Gatsby went along.

During his time with Cody, Gatsby had various roles. He worked as a steward, mate, skipper, secretary, and even a jailor. Cody knew that when he was drunk, he could get into trouble, so he trusted Gatsby to keep him out of trouble. This arrangement lasted for five years, during which the yacht traveled around the continent three times. It could have continued indefinitely, but one night in Boston, Ella Kaye came on board and a week later, Cody unfortunately passed away.

117   I remembered the portrait of him in Gatsby's bedroom, a gray, flushed man with a stern, vacant expression—an adventurer. Thanks to Cody, Gatsby rarely drank. It was also from Cody that Gatsby inherited money. It was wenty-five thousand dollars. Unfortunately, he never received it. He never quite grasped the legal scheme that

was used against him, but all of the remaining money went entirely to Ella Kaye. All he was left with was his somewhat appropriate education; the blurry image of Jay Gatsby transformed into the tangible form of a grown man.

❧

He shared all of this with me much later, but I'm including it here in order to cancel any rumors about his background that were completely untrue.

There was a pause in my involvement with his affairs. For a few weeks, I didn't see him or hear from him over the phone—I was mostly in New York, spending time with Jordan and trying to get in good with her elderly aunt. But eventually, I went to his house one Sunday afternoon. I had only been there for a couple of minutes when someone brought Tom Buchanan in for a drink. I was surprised, of course, but what was really shocking was that it hadn't happened earlier.

They were a group of three on horseback—Tom, a man named Sloane, and a pretty woman in a brown riding outfit who had visited before.

"I'm happy to see you," Gatsby said, standing on his porch. "I'm glad you stopped by."

As if they cared!

"Please, have a seat. Would you like a cigarette or a cigar?" He quickly walked around the room, ringing bells for the servants. "I'll have a drink ready for you in just a minute."

Tom's presence deeply affected him. Still, he would be restless until he had offered them something, realizing in a vague manner that it was all they came for. Mr. Sloane didn't want anything. A lemonade? No, thank you. A little champagne? None at all, thank you... I apologize—

"Did you have a nice ride?"

"The roads around here are very good."

"I suppose the automobiles—"

"Yeah."

Driven by an uncontrollable urge, Gatsby turned to Tom, who had accepted the introduction as if they were strangers.

"I believe we've crossed paths before, Mr. Buchanan."

"Oh, yes," said Tom, politely but gruffly, clearly not remembering. "So we did. I remember very well."

"About two weeks ago."

"That's right. You were with Nick here."

"I know your wife," Gatsby continued, almost aggressively.

"Is that so?"

Tom turned to me.

"You live nearby, Nick?"

"Next door."

"Is that so?"

Mr. Sloane didn't participate in the conversation, but instead sat back arrogantly in his chair. The woman remained silent as well, until unexpectedly, after two highballs, she became very, very friendly.

"We should all come to your next party, Mr. Gatsby," she suggested. "What do you say?"

"Certainly, I would be delighted to have you."

"That would be very nice," Mr. Sloane said, without gratitude. "Well, I think we should start heading home."

"Please don't rush," Gatsby urged them. He had regained control of himself and wanted to spend more time with Tom. "Why don't you... why don't you stay for dinner? I wouldn't be surprised if some other people from New York dropped by."

"Why don't you come have dinner with me?" the lady said enthusiastically. "Both of you."

This invitation included me. Mr. Sloane stood up.

"Come along," he said, but only to her.

"I really mean it," she insisted. "I would love to have you. We have plenty of space."

Gatsby looked at me questioningly. He wanted to go to dinner, but he didn't realize that Mr. Sloane had made up his mind that he shouldn't.

"I'm afraid I won't be able to," I said.

"Well, you should come," she urged, focusing on Gatsby.

Mr. Sloane muttered something close to her ear.

"We won't be late if we leave now," she insisted aloud.

"I don't own a horse," Gatsby stated. "I used to ride in the military, but I've never purchased a horse. I'll have to drive my car and follow you. Excuse me for a moment."

The rest of us walked out onto the porch, where Sloane and the lady began having a passionate conversation in private.

"Goodness gracious, I think that man is coming," Tom remarked. "Doesn't he realize that she doesn't want him?"

"She says she does want him."

"It's a large dinner party and he won't know anyone there." Tom frowned. "I wonder where on earth he met Daisy. By golly, I might have old-fashioned beliefs, but women are too active in these times for my liking. They meet all sorts of strange people."

Suddenly, Mr. Sloane and the lady descended the steps and mounted their horses.

"Let's go," Mr. Sloane said to Tom. "We're running late. We have to leave." And then to me: "Please inform him that we couldn't wait."

Tom and I shook hands, the rest of us exchanged a formal nod, and they quickly trotted down the driveway, disappearing beneath the lush August foliage just as Gatsby, carrying his hat and lightweight coat, emerged from the front door.

Tom seemed bothered by Daisy going out on her own because he accompanied her to Gatsby's party that following Saturday night. Everything was the same, but I felt an unpleasantness in the air. It's possible that I had grown accustomed to it, accepting West Egg as its own world with its unique standards and notable individuals, despite its lack of awareness of its significance. Now, I was seeing it through Daisy's perspective, which was sad because it makes you reconsider things that you had adapted to.

They arrived at dusk, and as we mingled among the sparkling crowd, Daisy's voice carried a soft tone.

"These things excite me," she sighed.

"Take a look around," Gatsby suggested.

"I am looking around. It's absolutely delightful—"

"You must recognize the faces of many people you've heard about."

Tom's arrogant gaze scanned the crowd.

"We don't really go out much," he said; "actually, I was just thinking that I don't know anyone here."

"Maybe you know that woman." Gatsby pointed to an amazingly beautiful woman who sat regally beneath a white plum tree. Tom and Daisy stared at her, feeling a strange sense of disbelief that comes when you recognize a famous person you've only seen on film.

"She's stunning," Daisy remarked.

"The man next to her is her director."

Gatsby guided them politely from one group to another.

"This is Mrs. Buchanan... and Mr. Buchanan," he said with a slight pause, "the polo player."

"Oh no," Tom objected quickly, "not me."

But Gatsby seemed to like the sound of it, so Tom remained "the polo player" for the rest of the evening.

"I've never met so many famous people," Daisy exclaimed. "I liked that man—what was his name?—with the blueish nose."

Gatsby identified him as a small film producer.

"Well, I liked him anyway."

"I would prefer not to be referred to as the polo player," Tom said pleasantly. "I would rather look at all these famous people from a distance."

Daisy and Gatsby danced together. I was surprised by how gracefully Gatsby danced, as I'd never seen his dancing skills before. Afterward, they walked over to my house and sat on the steps for about thirty minutes, while I kept a watchful eye on the garden as Daisy had requested. "Just in case there's a fire or a flood," she explained, "or any unforeseen event."

Tom interrupted our dinner. He asked, "Do you mind if I dine with some people over there? They're telling some funny stories."

"Go ahead," Daisy responded cheerfully. I could sense that she was not enjoying herself.

We were sitting at a rowdy table. I had previously found these people amusing just two weeks ago. However, what had entertained me back then now felt terrible now.

"How are you feeling, Miss Baedeker?"

The girl being addressed attempted, unsuccessfully, to slump against my shoulder. But upon hearing the question, she sat up and opened her eyes.

"What?"

A large and sluggish woman, who had been trying to convince Daisy to play golf with her at the local club tomorrow, spoke up to defend Miss Baedeker:

"Oh, she's fine now. When she's had five or six cocktails, she tends to start screaming like that. I keep telling her she should lay off."

"I do lay off," the accused responded hollowly.

"We heard you screaming, so I said to my friend here, 'Someone needs your help, Doc.'"

"She appreciates it, I'm sure," another friend sarcastically added, "but you did get her dress all wet when you dunked her head in the pool."

Their conversation continued. It was all very silly.

It was like that. The last thing I remember is standing with Daisy, watching the movie director and his star. They were still under the white plum tree, their faces close together except for a ray of moonlight between them. I realized that he had been slowly getting closer to her all evening, and while I watched, he leaned in and kissed her cheek.

"I like her," said Daisy. "I think she's beautiful."

But the rest of the situation bothered her—definitely because it wasn't just a gesture, but an emotion. She was shocked by West Egg, this new "place" that had been created by Broadway in a quiet fishing village on Long Island. She was appalled by the intense energy that clashed with the old ways of speaking and by the obvious fate that guided its residents towards emptiness. She saw something awful in the simplicity she couldn't comprehend.

125   I sat on the front steps with them while they waited for their car.

"Who is this Gatsby anyway?" Tom suddenly asked. "Is he some big-time illegal liquor dealer?"

"Where did you hear that?" I asked.

"I didn't hear it. I just thought of it. Many of these newly rich people are just illegal liquor dealers, you know."

"Not Gatsby," I quickly responded.

Tom stayed silent for a moment as he walked on the gravel driveway.

"Well, he must have gone to great lengths to gather this group of people together."

"At least they are more interesting than the people we know," Daisy said with some effort.

"You didn't seem too interested," Tom said, laughing, and then turned to me.

Daisy started to sing along with the music coming from the house. She was enchanting.

126   "Many people come to his parties without being invited," she said suddenly. "That girl wasn't invited. They just force their way in and he doesn't object because he's too polite."

"I want to know who he is and what he does," Tom insisted. "And I'm determined to find out."

"I can tell you right now," she replied. "He owned a bunch of drugstores. He built them up himself."

The slow limousine arrived, rolling up the driveway.

"Good night, Nick," said Daisy.

She looked away from me and stared at the illumination at the top of the steps. The sound of "Three O'Clock in the Morning," a gentle and melancholy waltz from that year, drifted through the open door. Despite the casualness of Gatsby's party, there were romantic possibilities that didn't exist in her own world. What was it about that song that seemed to draw her back inside? What would happen during the uncertain hours of the night? Maybe an extraordinary guest would arrive, someone incredibly special and captivating, a truly radiant young woman who, with just one glance at Gatsby, one magical moment, would erase those five years of unwavering loyalty.

I stayed late that night. Gatsby asked me to wait until he had finished his responsibilities, and I remained in the garden until the predictable swimming gathering had ended, with everyone feeling invigorated and chilled after their time at the dark beach, and the lights were turned off in the rooms where the guests stayed. Finally, when he descended the stairs, his sun-kissed complexion appeared especially tight on his face, and his eyes seemed both lively and weary.

"She didn't enjoy herself," he immediately expressed.

"Of course she did."

"No, she didn't," he insisted. "She didn't have a good time."

He fell silent, and I could sense his indescribable sense of sadness.

"I feel distant from her," he said. "It's difficult for me to make her understand."

"Are you referring to the dance?"

"The dance?" He dismissed all the dances he had organized with a dismissive gesture. "Old sport, the dance doesn't matter."

He desired nothing less from Daisy than for her to approach Tom and declare: "I never loved you." Once she had erased four years with that declaration, they could then plan out the more practical steps to be taken. One of those steps was that, once she was free, they would return to Louisville and get married at her house—as if it were five years ago.

"And she doesn't understand," he said. "She used to be capable of understanding. We would sit for hours—"

He abruptly stopped and began pacing along a dreary path covered in discarded fruit rinds, party favors, and crushed flowers.

"I wouldn't ask too much of her," I suggested cautiously. "You can't recreate the past."

"Can't repeat the past?" he exclaimed with disbelief. "Well, of course you can!"

He looked around anxiously, as if the past were hiding here in the darkness of his house, just out of his grasp.

"I'm going to restore everything to how it was before," he declared, nodding determinedly. "She'll see."

He spoke extensively about the past, and I gathered that he longed to retrieve something, perhaps a sense of himself, that he had lost in loving Daisy. His life had been chaotic and disordered since then, but if he could only return to a specific starting point and revisit it slowly, he believed he could uncover the significance of that something...

... Several years ago, during an autumn evening, they were strolling down the street as leaves cascaded down, and they reached a spot where no trees stood, and the moonlight bathed the sidewalk in a soft glow. They paused there and turned towards each other. Now it was a crisp night, filled with that mysterious thrill that accompanies the transitions between seasons. The quiet lights emanating from the houses were murmuring into the darkness, and there was commotion and liveliness among the stars. From the corner of his eye, Gatsby noticed that the blocks of the sidewalk seemed to form a ladder, leading to a secret place above the trees. He realized that he could climb it, if he went alone, and once there, he could taste the essence of life, drink down the extraordinary nectar of marvel.

His heart raced as Daisy's pale face approached his own. He knew that when he kissed this girl and committed himself to her fleeting breath, his mind would never soar again like the divine mind. So he waited, listening a little longer to the celestial music that had resonated within him. Then he kissed her. At the touch of his lips, she blossomed like a delicate flower, and their union was complete.

Despite his overly sentimental demeanor, everything he said evoked a familiar melody, a fragment of forgotten words that I had encountered long ago. For a moment, a phrase attempted to form on my lips, and they parted hesitantly, as if they held more than just a gasp of astonishment. But no sound emerged, and the ungraspable memory was forever unexpressed.

CHAPTER

SEVEN

130   DURING THE PEAK of curiosity surrounding Gatsby, the lights in his house unexpectedly remained dark on a Saturday night. Just as mysteriously as it had begun, his extravagant lifestyle as Trimalchio came to an end. It slowly became apparent that the cars that eagerly entered his driveway merely stayed for a brief moment before departing with disappointment. Concerned about his well-being, I decided to check on him. An unfamiliar butler with a dubious expression stared at me suspiciously from the doorway.

"Is Mr. Gatsby unwell?"

"Nope." After a brief pause, he grudgingly added, "Sir."

"I haven't seen him lately, and it got me worried. Please let him know that Mr. Carraway came by."

"Who?" he rudely demanded.

"Carraway."

"Carraway. Alright, I'll pass along the message."

He abruptly slammed the door shut.

Later, my housekeeper informed me that Gatsby had dismissed all of his servants a week prior and replaced them with a handful of others who never ventured into West Egg village to avoid being bribed by local traders. Instead, they ordered basic supplies over the telephone. The boy from the grocery store mentioned that the kitchen appeared unkempt, and the general consensus in the village was that these new individuals were not genuine servants at all.

The following day, Gatsby contacted me via telephone.

"Are you planning a trip?" I inquired.

"No, old friend."

"I heard you let go of all your staff."

"I wanted someone who wouldn't engage in idle gossip. Daisy visits frequently—in the afternoons."

The whole caravansary had collapsed like a flimsy house of cards when she disapproved.

"They're some people Wolfshiem wanted to help. They're all siblings. They used to manage a small hotel."

"I understand."

He called at Daisy's request—would I come to her house for lunch tomorrow? Miss Baker would be there. Half an hour later, Daisy herself called and seemed relieved to hear that I was coming. Something was going on. And yet, I couldn't believe that they would choose this occasion for a confrontation—especially the intense one that Gatsby had described in the garden.

The following day was scorching, almost the last and definitely the hottest day of the summer. As my train emerged from the tunnel into the sunlight, only the loud whistles of the National Biscuit Company disrupted the simmering silence at noon. The straw seats in the train car seemed on the verge of catching fire; the woman beside me perspired lightly onto her white blouse for a while, and then, as her newspaper grew damp under her fingers, she helplessly succumbed to the intense heat with a despairing cry. Her purse fell to the floor.

"Oh, my!" she gasped.

I wearily picked it up and handed it back to her, holding it at arm's length and only by the very edges to show that I had no intentions of taking it—but everyone nearby, including the woman, still suspected me.

"It's scorching!" the conductor exclaimed to familiar faces. "This weather is unbearable! Is it too hot for you?"

After he took my train ticket and punched it, he returned it to me. It was wet with sweat.

A faint breeze blew through the hallway of the Buchanan house.

He approached us, glistening with sweat.

"Madam is expecting you in the living room!" he exclaimed unnecessarily, pointing the way.

The room, shaded by awnings, was dim and cool. Daisy and Jordan sat on the couch.

"We can't even move," they said in unison. I heard Tom on the phone in the hallway.

Gatsby stood in the middle of the red carpet and looked around with fascinated eyes. Daisy watched him and laughed, her sweet, exciting laugh; a small puff of powder rose from her chest into the air.

"The word is," whispered Jordan, "that that's Tom's girl on the phone."

We were quiet. The voice in the hallway rose with annoyance: "Okay, fine, then I won't sell you the car at all... I don't owe you anything... and don't bother me about it during lunchtime, I won't tolerate that!"

"Holding down the receiver," said Daisy cynically.

"No, he's not," I assured her. "It's a real deal. I happen to know about it."

Tom flung open the door, briefly blocking its space with his solid body, and hurried into the room.

"Mr. Gatsby!" He reached out his broad, flat hand with well-hidden dislike. "I'm glad to see you, sir... Nick..."

"Make us a cold drink," cried Daisy.

As he left the room again, she got up and went to Gatsby, pulling his face down and kissing him on the mouth.

"You know I love you," she whispered.

"You forget there's a lady here," said Jordan.

Daisy looked around doubtfully.

"Kiss Nick too."

"What an uncouth girl!"

"I don't care!" cried Daisy, and began to tap dance on the brick fireplace. Then she remembered the heat and sat down guiltily on the couch just as a freshly washed nurse leading a little girl entered the room.

"Sweet little one," she sang softly, extending her arms. "Come to your dear mother who loves you."

The child, released by the nurse, hurriedly crossed the room and timidly clung to her mother's dress.

"My sweet darling! Did Mama get powder on your old yellowy hair? Stand up now and say, 'Howdy-do.'"

Gatsby and I, one by one, stooped down and held the small, hesitant hand. Later, he continued to gaze at the child in astonishment. I don't think he had ever truly believed in her existence before.

"I got dressed before lunch," the child shared eagerly, turning towards Daisy.

"That's because your mother wanted to proudly show you off." Daisy's face wrinkled with affection as she kissed the child's small, pale neck. "You are a dream, my love. An absolute little dream."

"Yes," the child calmly admitted. "Aunt Jordan is also wearing a white dress."

"How do you like Mother's friends?" Daisy turned the child to face Gatsby. "Do you think they're beautiful?"

"Where's Daddy?"

"She doesn't resemble her father," Daisy explained. "She looks like me. She has my hair and the shape of my face."

Daisy settled back on the sofa. The nurse stepped forward and reached out her hand.

"Come along, Pammy."

"Goodbye, sweetheart!"

With a hesitant glance backward, the well-behaved child held onto her nurse's hand and was led out the door, just as Tom returned carrying four gin rickeys filled with ice that clinked together.

Gatsby picked up his drink.

"They certainly appear refreshing," he remarked, visibly tense.

We gulped down our drinks eagerly.

"I remember reading somewhere that the sun is getting hotter every year," Tom said cheerfully. "It's like the Earth is going to end up falling into the sun, or wait a minute, it's the opposite, the sun is actually getting colder every year."

"Why don't we go outside?" Tom suggested to Gatsby. "I want you to see the place."

I joined them on the porch. In the sweltering heat, a small sailboat crept slowly towards the cooler sea. Gatsby briefly followed it with his eyes, then raised his hand and pointed across the bay.

"I live right across from you."

"So you do."

Our gaze drifted over the rose beds, the scorching lawn, and the litter left by the summer days along the shore. The white wings of the boat moved slowly against the vast blue sky. Beyond lay the curved ocean and the beautiful islands.

"Now that's a way to have fun," Tom remarked, nodding. "I'd love to be out there for an hour."

We had lunch in the dimly lit dining room, trying to escape from the heat, and chased away our nervousness with cold ale.

"What should we do this afternoon?" Daisy exclaimed. "And the day after that, and the next thirty years?"

"Don't be morbid," Jordan responded. "Life starts anew when fall arrives and the air turns crisp."

"But it's so hot," Daisy insisted, her voice trembling on the verge of tears. "And everything is so chaotic. Let's all go to the city!"

Her voice fought through the oppressive heat, struggling to make sense of the confusion.

"I've heard about people turning stables into garages," Tom said to Gatsby. "But I'm the first person who turned a garage into a stable."

"Who wants to go to the city?" Daisy demanded, insistent. Gatsby's eyes drifted towards her. "Oh," she exclaimed, "you look so calm."

Their eyes met, and they gazed at each other, alone in their own world. With some effort, Daisy looked down at the table.

"You always seem so composed," she repeated.

She had confessed her love to him, and Tom Buchanan noticed. He was astonished. His mouth slightly opened, and he glanced at Gatsby, then back at Daisy as if he had just recognized her from a long time ago.

"You resemble that man from the advertisement," she continued innocently. "You know, the one in the advertisement—"

"Alright," interrupted Tom quickly. "I'm perfectly fine with going to the city. Come on, we're all going to the city."

He stood up, his eyes still flickering between Gatsby and his wife. No one moved.

"Come on!" His temper cracked a little. "What's the matter, anyway? If we're going to the city, let's get going."

His hand, shaking with his attempt to control himself, brought the last sip of his glass of ale to his lips. Daisy's voice prompted us to rise from our seats and exit onto the scorching gravel driveway.

"Are we just leaving?" she objected. "Like this? Aren't we going to let anyone smoke a cigarette first?"

"Everyone smoked all throughout lunch."

"Oh, let's have some fun," she pleaded with him. "It's too hot to argue."

He didn't respond.

"Sure, have it your way," she said. "Come on, Jordan."

They went upstairs to get ready while the three of us stood there shuffling the hot pebbles with our feet. A sliver of the moon was already hovering high in the western sky. Gatsby started to speak, then changed his mind. But not before Tom turned around and faced him, expecting an answer.

"Do you have your horses here?" Gatsby asked, making an effort.

"They're about a quarter of a mile down the road."

"Oh."

There was a pause.

"I don't understand why we're going to town," Tom burst out angrily. "Women get these ideas in their heads—"

"Should we bring something to drink?" Daisy called from an upstairs window.

"I'll get some whiskey," Tom replied, and went inside.

Gatsby turned to me stiffly.

"I can't say anything in his house, old sport."

"She has a loud voice," I commented. "It's full of—" I hesitated.

"Her voice is full of money," he suddenly said.

That was it. I had never understood before. It was full of money, that was the endless charm that rang through it and faded away, the sound of coins, the melody of riches... Up in a white palace, the king's daughter, the golden girl...

Tom came out of the house with a quart bottle wrapped in a towel, followed by Daisy and Jordan who were wearing small hats made of shiny fabric and carrying lightweight capes over their arms.

"How about we all go in my car?" Gatsby suggested. He felt the hot, green leather of the seat. "I should have left it in the shade."

"Is it a manual transmission?" Tom asked.

"Well, you can take my car and I'll drive yours instead," Tom suggested.

Gatsby didn't like this idea.

"I don't think I have much gas," he objected.

"We have plenty of gas," Tom said loudly. He checked the gauge. "And if we run out, we can stop at a drugstore. You can buy anything at a drugstore nowadays."

There was a brief silence following this seemingly random remark. Daisy looked at Tom with a frown, and a familiar yet unfamiliar expression crossed Gatsby's face, as if I had only heard it described in words.

"Come on, Daisy," said Tom, nudging her towards Gatsby's car. "I'll take you in this fancy ride."

He opened the door, but she pulled away from him.

"You go with Nick and Jordan. We'll follow you in the coupe."

She walked close to Gatsby, lightly touching his coat with her hand.

"Did you see that?" Tom asked. He scrutinized me, realizing that Jordan and I must have known all along.

"You probably think I'm not very smart, right?" he suggested. "I have senses though. I sense something now."

He stopped himself and pulled himself back from the edge.

"I've done a little investigation on this guy," he continued. "I could have looked deeper if I had known—"

"Do you mean you've been to see a psychic?" asked Jordan jokingly.

"What?" Confused, he looked at us as we laughed. "A psychic?"

"About Gatsby."

"About Gatsby! No, I haven't. I said I've been looking into his past."

"And you found out he went to Oxford," said Jordan helpfully.

"An Oxford man!" He couldn't believe it. "No way! He wears a pink suit."

"Still, he is an Oxford man."

"Oxford, New Mexico," scoffed Tom disdainfully, "or something like that."

"Listen, Tom. If you're such a snob, why did you invite him to lunch?" demanded Jordan angrily.

"Daisy invited him; she knew him before we got married—Heaven knows where!"

We were all getting annoyed now with the fading gas, and aware of it we drove in silence for a while. Then, as we saw Doctor T. J.

Eckleburg's worn-out eyes in the distance, I remembered Gatsby's warning about running out of gas.

"We have enough to get us to town," said Tom.

"But there's a gas station right here," objected Jordan. "I don't want to get stuck in this sweltering heat."

Tom slammed on the brakes impatiently, and we came to a sudden dusty stop under Wilson's sign. After a moment, the owner came out from inside his shop and looked at the car with empty eyes.

"Let's get some gas!" yelled Tom rudely. "Why do you think we stopped—for the view?"

"I feel sick," Wilson said without moving. "I've been feeling sick all day."

"What's wrong?"

"I'm exhausted."

"Well, can I help myself?" Tom asked impatiently. "You sounded fine on the phone."

With some effort, Wilson stepped out of the shade and let go of the door for support. He unscrewed the cap of the gas tank, breathing heavily. In the sunlight, his face looked pale.

"I didn't mean to interrupt your lunch," he said. "But I really need some money right now, and I was wondering what you were planning to do with your old car."

"How do you like this one?" Tom asked. "I bought it just last week."

"It's a nice yellow car," replied Wilson as he strained to turn the handle.

"Interested in buying it?"

"Not really," Wilson weakly smiled. "But I could make some money by selling the other one."

"Why do you suddenly need money?"

"I've been stuck here for too long. I want to leave. My wife and I want to go out West."

"Your wife?" Tom exclaimed, surprised.

"She's been talking about it for ten years," Wilson said, pausing to rest against the gas pump and shielding his eyes from the sun. "And now she's leaving, whether she wants to or not. I'm going to take her away."

The coupe passed us quickly, leaving behind a trail of dust and a waving hand.

"How much do I owe you?" Tom demanded harshly.

"Something strange has been going on the past two days," Wilson began. "That's why I need to get away. That's why I've been bothering you about the car."

"How much do I owe you?"

"A dollar twenty."

141 The intense heat was starting to confuse me. I panicked before realizing that Tom had not yet become the target of suspicions. Wilson had discovered that Myrtle had a life separate from him in another world,. This shock had made him physically ill. I stared at Wilson and then at Tom, who had made a similar discovery just an hour earlier. It dawned on me that there was no greater difference between people, regardless of intelligence or race, than the distinction between those who were sick and those who were well. Wilson looked so ill that he appeared guilty, unforgivably guilty—as if he had just impregnated a young woman.

"I'll let you have the car," Tom offered. "I'll arrange for it to be delivered tomorrow afternoon."

That part of town had always made me somewhat uneasy, even in the bright light of afternoon. Now, as if warned of something lurking behind me, I turned my head. Above the piles of ashes, the enormous eyes of Doctor T. J. Eckleburg kept a watchful gaze. But after a moment, I realized that there were other eyes intensely observing us from a distance of less than twenty feet.

142 In one of the windows above the garage, the curtains were slightly moved and Myrtle Wilson was peering down at the car. She was so engrossed in her observation that she didn't realize she was being watched. Various emotions flickered across her face, gradually forming a picture. Her expression was oddly familiar, one that I had

seen on women before. However, on Myrtle Wilson's face, it seemed aimless and inexplicable until I realized that her wide eyes, filled with jealous terror, were not fixed on Tom, but on Jordan Baker, whom she mistook for his wife.

THERE IS no confusion quite like the confusion of a simple mind. As we drove away, Tom was overwhelmed by a wave of panic. His wife and his mistress, previously secure and untouchable, were slipping out of his grip. Instinct compelled him to press on the accelerator, both to catch up to Daisy and to leave Wilson behind. We raced towards Astoria at fifty miles per hour, until we caught sight of the relaxed blue coupé among the intricate framework of the elevated train tracks.

"Those big movies near Fiftieth Street are great," Jordan suggested. "I love New York on summer afternoons when everyone is away. There's something very senusous about it, as if all kinds of amusing possibilities were within your reach."

The word "sensuous" made Tom even more uneasy, but before he could voice his objection, the car came to a stop, and Daisy gestured for us to pull up beside her.

"Where are we going?" she exclaimed.

"What about going to the movies?"

"It's so hot," she complained. "Why don't you go? We'll drive around and meet you later." She managed to come up with a clever idea. "We'll meet you at a street corner. I'll be the one smoking two cigarettes."

"We can't argue about it here," Tom said impatiently, as a truck honked behind us. "Follow me to the south side of Central Park, in front of the Plaza Hotel."

Several times, he glanced back, searching for their car. Whenever traffic slowed them down, he would reduce speed until they came into view. I believe he was afraid they would suddenly turn into a side street and disappear from his life forever.

But they didn't. And we all made the perplexing decision to rent a room in the parlor of a suite at the Plaza Hotel.

The long, loud argument that ended with us being pushed into that room is a bit fuzzy in my memory. It was so very hot. Daisy suggested finding a place to have mint juleps.

The room we got was large and stuffy. Daisy went to the mirror and stood with her back to us, fixing her hair.

"It's a nice suite," Jordan whispered respectfully, and everyone laughed.

"Daisy, why don't you open another window?" Tom asked, but Daisy didn't turn around.

"There aren't any more windows."

"Well, we might as well call for an axe then—"

"Complaining about the heat only makes it worse," Tom interrupted.

"Why don't you leave her alone, old sport?" Gatsby said. "You're the one who wanted to come to town."

There was a moment of silence.

"I can grab it," I offered.

"No need, I've got it." Gatsby examined the frayed string, muttered "Hmm!" with interest, and casually tossed the book onto a chair.

"That catchphrase of yours, 'old sport,' is quite something, isn't it?" Tom said sharply.

"What do you mean?"

"All this 'old sport' talk. Where did you learn that?"

"Now wait a minute, Tom," Daisy said, turning away from the mirror. "If you're going to make personal comments, I won't stay here for another minute. Call and order some ice for the mint juleps."

As Tom picked up the phone, the stifling heat suddenly erupted into sound, and we found ourselves listening to the grand chords of Mendelssohn's Wedding March from the ballroom below.

"Can you believe getting married in this heat?" Jordan said sadly.

"Well, I got married in the middle of June," Daisy recalled. "Louisville in June! Someone fainted. Who was it, Tom?"

"Biloxi," he answered curtly.

"A man named Biloxi. They called him 'Blocks' Biloxi, and he made boxes, true story, and he was from Biloxi, Tennessee."

"They carried him into my house," added Jordan, "because we lived just two doors down from the church. And he stayed for three weeks, until my dad told him to leave. The day after he left, my dad passed away." After a moment, she added, "There was no connection between the two events."

"I used to know a Bill Biloxi from Memphis," I commented.

"That was his cousin. I knew his entire family history before he left. He even gave me an aluminum putter that I still use today."

The music had faded as the ceremony started and now a loud cheer floated through the window, followed by occasional shouts of "Yeah" and finally by a burst of lively music as the dancing began.

"We're getting older," Daisy remarked. "If we were young, we would get up and dance."

"Remember Biloxi," Jordan reminded her. "Where did you know him, Tom?"

"Biloxi?" Tom struggled to remember. "I didn't know him. He was a friend of Daisy's."

"No, he wasn't," Daisy denied. "I had never seen him before. He arrived in a private car."

"Well, he claimed to know you. He said he was raised in Louisville. Asa Bird brought him around at the last minute and asked if we had space for him."

Jordan smiled.

"He was probably hitchhiking his way home. He told me he was the president of your class at Yale."

Tom and I exchanged puzzled looks.

"Biloxi?"

"First of all, we didn't have a president—"

Gatsby's foot tapped out a restless beat and Tom suddenly eyed him.

"By the way, Mr. Gatsby, I heard you're an Oxford man."

"Not exactly."

"Oh, yes, I heard you went to Oxford."

"Yes, I did attend there."

A moment of silence. Then Tom's voice, disbelieving and insulting: "You must have gone there around the same time Biloxi went to New Haven."

Another pause. A waiter knocked and entered with crushed mint and ice, but the silence remained unbroken by his "thank you" and the gentle closing of the door. This significant detail was about to be clarified once and for all.

"I told you I went there," Gatsby said.

"I heard you, but I would like to know when."

"It was in 1919, I only stayed for five months. That's why I can't really say I'm an Oxford man."

Tom looked at each of us to see if we shared his disbelief. However, we were all fixated on Gatsby.

"They offered this opportunity to some of the officers after the armistice," he continued. "We could choose any of the universities in England or France."

I felt an urge to give him a pat on the back. I had that renewed sense of complete faith in him that I had felt before.

Daisy stood up, smiling faintly, and went to the table.

"Open the whiskey, Tom," she ordered, "and I'll make you a mint julep. Then you won't feel so foolish... Look at the mint!"

"Just hold on a minute," snapped Tom, "I want to ask Mr. Gatsby one more question."

"Go ahead," Gatsby responded politely.

"What kind of trouble are you trying to cause in my house?"

They were finally addressing the issue openly, and Gatsby seemed satisfied.

"He isn't causing trouble," Daisy pleaded, looking desperately at both of them. "You're the one causing trouble. Please show some self-control."

"Self-control!" echoed Tom in disbelief. "I suppose the trend nowadays is to sit back and let some nobody from nowhere flirt with your wife. Well, if that's the idea, you can count me out... Nowadays, people start by mocking family life and institutions, and next thing you know, they'll throw everything away and start promoting marriages between black and white."

148

With his passionate rambling, he imagined himself standing alone on the final edge of society.

"We're all white here," muttered Jordan.

"I know I'm not very popular. I don't throw big parties. I guess you have to turn your house into a mess to have any friends in today's world."

As angry as I was, as we all were, I couldn't help but want to laugh whenever he spoke. The transformation from a pleasure-seeker to a self-righteous person was so complete.

"I have something to tell you, my friend—" Gatsby started. But Daisy understood his intention.

"Please, don't!" she interrupted helplessly. "Let's all go home. Why don't we just go home?"

"That's a good idea," I stood up. "Come on, Tom. Nobody wants a drink."

"I want to know what Mr. Gatsby has to say to me."

"Your wife doesn't love you," stated Gatsby. "She's never loved you. She loves me."

"You must be insane!" exclaimed Tom instinctively.

Gatsby jumped up, filled with excitement.

"She never loved you, do you hear?" he shouted. "She only married you because I was poor and she grew tired of waiting for me. It was a terrible mistake, but deep down in her heart, she never loved anyone except me!"

At this point, Jordan and I attempted to leave, but both Tom and Gatsby firmly insisted that we stay--as if neither of them had anything to hide and it would be an honor to experience their emotions vicariously.

"Please have a seat, Daisy," Tom's voice attempted to sound authoritative. "What's been happening? I want to hear all about it."

"I already told you what's been happening," Gatsby replied. "It's been going on for five years—and you were clueless."

Tom turned to Daisy with a sharp look.

"You've been seeing this guy for five years?"

"Not seeing," Gatsby clarified. "No, we couldn't meet. But both of us loved each other all that time, my friend, and you had no idea. Sometimes I used to laugh"—but there was no laughter in his eyes—"thinking about how oblivious you were."

"Oh, is that all? You're delusional!" he burst out. "I can't discuss what happened five years ago since I didn't know Daisy back then. I'm not even sure how you could have gotten so close unless you were delivering groceries through the back door. You're a liar though. Daisy loved me when she married me, and she loves me now."

"No," Gatsby shook his head.

"But she does. The problem is that sometimes she gets foolish notions in her head and acts without thinking," Tom sagely nodded. "And moreover, I love Daisy too. Every now and then, I may embark on reckless endeavors and make a fool of myself, but I always return, and deep down, I love her."

"You're disgusting," Daisy remarked with disdain. She turned towards me, her voice lowering in pitch, as she filled the room with scornful words. "Do you know why we left Chicago? I'm surprised they didn't tell you about that little episode."

Gatsby approached and stood beside Daisy.

"Daisy, that's all in the past now," he said earnestly. "It doesn't matter anymore. Just tell him the truth--that you never loved him-- and it will all be forgotten."

She looked at him, lost and uncertain. "Why... how could I possibly love him?"

"You never loved him."

She hesitated, her gaze shifting towards Jordan and me, almost as if she finally realized the consequences of her actions--as if she had never intended to do anything at all. But it was too late. It had been done.

"I never loved him," she reluctantly admitted.

"Not even at Kapiolani?" Tom suddenly asked.

"No."

From below, the sounds of muffled music drifted upwards on the stifling air.

"Not even on the day I carried you from the Punch Bowl to keep your shoes dry?" His tone held a husky tenderness. "Daisy?"

"Please, stop," she replied, her voice now devoid of bitterness. She looked at Gatsby. "There, Jay," she said, but her hand trembled as she attempted to light a cigarette. Without warning, she hurled the cigarette and the burning match onto the carpet.

"You're asking for too much!" exclaimed Daisy to Gatsby. "I love you now, isn't that enough? I can't change the past." She started crying uncontrollably. "I did love him once, but I loved you too."

Gatsby blinked his eyes.

"You loved me too?" he repeated.

"Even that's not true," said Tom angrily. "She didn't even know you were alive. There are things between Daisy and me that you'll never understand, things we can never forget."

Gatsby wanted to talk to Daisy alone.

"You don't understand," said Gatsby, with a hint of panic. "You can't take care of her anymore."

"I can't?" Tom widened his eyes and laughed. He could control himself now. "Why is that?"

"Daisy is leaving you."

"Absurd."

"But I am," she said, struggling to speak.

"She's not leaving me!" Tom's words loomed over Gatsby. "Certainly not for a common fraud who had to steal the ring he put on her finger."

"I can't tolerate this!" cried Daisy. "Oh, please, let's leave."

"Who are you anyway?" demanded Tom. "You're part of that group that hangs around with Meyer Wolfshiem. I found out what your 'drugstores' were all about." He turned to us and spoke quickly. "He and this Wolfshiem guy bought up a bunch of little drugstores in this area and in Chicago, and they sold illegal alcohol to people. That's one of his tricks. The first time I saw him, I knew he was involved in bootlegging, and I wasn't too far off."

"So what?" replied Gatsby politely. "I think your friend Walter Chase didn't hesitate to join in."

"Yeah, and you left him high and dry, didn't you? You let him end up in jail for a month in New Jersey. You should hear what Walter thinks of you, my God!"

"He was completely broke when he came to us. He was thrilled to have the opportunity to make some money, old sport."

"Don't call me 'old sport'!" shouted Tom. Gatsby remained silent. "Walter could expose you for breaking the betting laws as well, but Wolfshiem scared him into keeping quiet."

That unfamiliar yet familiar expression returned to Gatsby's face.

"That drugstore scheme was just a small part of it," Tom continued slowly. "But now you're involved in something that even Walter is scared to tell me about."

I glanced at Daisy, who was staring fearfully between Gatsby and her husband, and at Jordan.

That moment passed, and Gatsby began to speak anxiously to Daisy, denying everything, defending his reputation. But with each word she pulled away. His dream was slipping from his grip.

"Please, Tom! I can't handle this anymore."

Her frightened eyes revealed that whatever plans or courage she had was gone

"You two go home, Daisy," said Tom. "In Mr. Gatsby's car."

She looked at Tom, now alarmed, but he insisted. "Go ahead. He won't bother you. I think he understands that this is finished."

They left without a word.

After a moment, Tom stood up and began wrapping the unopened bottle of whiskey in a towel.

"Do any of you want this? Jordan?... Nick?"

I didn't respond.

"No... I just remembered that today is my birthday."

I was thirty years old. Ahead of me was the ominous road of a new decade.

It was seven o'clock when we got into the car with him and started driving towards Long Island. Tom talked nonstop, feeling triumphant and laughing, but his voice felt distant to Jordan and me, like the foreign noise on the sidewalk or the chaos of the elevated train above. There are limits to human empathy, and we were content to let their tragic arguments fade away as the city lights disappeared behind us. Thirty years old—a promise of ten years of solitude, a diminishing number of single men to meet, a dwindling amount of enthusiasm and thinning hair. But Jordan was next to me and, unlike Daisy, she was too wise to hold onto forgotten dreams from one age to another. As we crossed the dark bridge, her tired face leaned lazily against my shoulder, and the weight of turning thirty diminished with the comforting touch of her hand.

So we drove on toward death through the cooling twilight.

THE YOUNG GREEK MAN, Michaelis, who ran the coffee shop next to the piles of ashes, was the main witness in the investigation. He had slept until after five because of the heat. Then he walked over to the garage and found George Wilson feeling very sick in his office. Wilson was pale, like his own pale hair, and trembling all over. Michaelis suggested that he go to bed, but Wilson refused, saying that he would miss out on a lot of business if he did. While his neighbor tried to convince him otherwise, a loud commotion erupted upstairs.

"I have my wife locked up there," Wilson calmly explained.

"She's going to stay there until the day after tomorrow, and then we're going to move away."

Michaelis was surprised; they had been neighbors for four years, and Wilson had never seemed even remotely capable of making such a statement. Usually, he was one of those exhausted men: when he wasn't working, he sat on a chair in the doorway and gazed at the people and cars passing by. Whenever someone spoke to him, he always laughed in a pleasant, unexciting manner. He was more devoted to his wife than to himself.

Determined to learn what had happened, Michaelis tried to press Wilson for information, but Wilson refused to speak and instead grew suspicious of his visitor, questioning him about his whereabouts on specific days. Just as Michaelis started to feel uneasy, some workers walked by on their way to the restaurant, offering him an opportunity to leave. He planned to return later, but he must have forgotten. When he stepped outside again, a little past seven, he overheard Mrs. Wilson's loud, scolding voice coming from the garage below.

He heard her scream, "Hit me! Throw me down and hit me, you coward!"

Moments later, Mrs. Wilson emerged from the darkness, wildly waving her hands and yelling. Before he could react, the incident was over.

The "death car," as described by the newspapers, did not stop. It emerged from the growing darkness, wavered for a brief moment, and then vanished around the bend. Michaelis couldn't even confirm its color—he initially told the first policeman it was light green. The other car, traveling towards New York, stopped a hundred yards ahead, and the driver hurried back to the lifeless body of Myrtle Wilson, her dark blood mixing with the dust on the road.

Michaelis and another man got to her first, but when they had opened her soaked shirt, they saw that her left breast was hanging limply like a loose flap, and they didn't need to listen for her heartbeat. Her mouth was wide open and torn at the edges, as if she had choked while giving up all the vitality she had held onto for so long.

~

WE NOTICED the few cars and the gathering of people from a distance.

"Accident!" Tom exclaimed. "That's interesting. Wilson might have some business now."

He slowed down, but had no intention of stopping until, as we approached closer, the serious, focused expressions on the faces of the individuals at the garage entrance made him instinctively hit the brakes.

"We should take a look," he said hesitantly, "just to see what's going on."

Now, I became aware of a hollow, mournful sound coming from the garage, a sound that, as we stepped out of the car and walked towards the door, formed itself into the words "Oh, my God!" repeatedly uttered in a desperate whimper.

"There's a terrible problem here," said Tom, filled with excitement.

He stood up on his toes and peered over a group of heads into the dimly lit garage, illuminated only by a yellow light hanging from a swinging metal basket above. Then he let out a harsh noise from his throat and forcefully pushed his way through with a powerful motion of his arms.

The group closed in again with a murmuring of disapproval. It took a moment before I could see anything. We were all pushed inside.

Myrtle Wilson's body was on a table against the wall, covered in blankets as if she were cold in the hot night. Tom stood by her, facing away from us, unmoving. Beside him, a motorcycle policeman diligently took names, sweating and making corrections in a small book. I spotted Wilson standing in the doorway of his office, swaying as he held onto the doorposts with both hands. Another man was speaking to him quietly, occasionally trying to touch his shoulder. Wilson didn't hear or see him. Wilson's gaze was all over. He cried and cried.

"Oh, my God! Oh, my God! Oh, God! Oh, my God!"

Suddenly, Tom raised his head abruptly. After staring around the garage with unfocused eyes, he muttered an incoherent remark to the policeman.

"M-a-v..." the policeman started saying, "...o..."

"No, r—" the man corrected him, "M-a-v-r-o—"

"Listen to me!" Tom grumbled fiercely.

"r—" said the policeman, "o—"

"What happened? That's what I want to know."

"A car hit her. Killed her instantly."

"Instantly killed," Tom repeated, staring.

"She ran out into the road. The driver didn't even stop the car."

"There were two cars," Michaelis said, "one coming, one going, you see?"

"Where was it going?" the policeman asked, interested.

"One going each way. Well, she--" His hand gestured towards the blankets but stopped halfway and dropped to his side. "--she ran out there, and the car coming from New York hit her, going about thirty or forty miles per hour."

"What's the name of this place?" the officer demanded.

"It doesn't have a name."

A pale, well-dressed African American man approached.

"It was a yellow car," he said, "a big, yellow car. Brand new."

"Did you witness the accident?" the policeman asked.

"No, but the car passed me down the road, going way faster than forty. Maybe fifty, sixty."

"Come here, let's get your name. Be careful now. I need to know his name."

Some words from this conversation must have reached Wilson, swaying in the doorway of his office, because suddenly a new topic emerged amidst his desperate cries:

"You don't have to tell me what kind of car it was! I know what kind of car it was!"

Observing Tom, I noticed the tension in the muscles behind his shoulder, visible even under his coat. He swiftly walked over to Wilson and, standing in front of him, firmly grasped his upper arms.

"You need to compose yourself," he said, trying to sound comforting and stern at the same time.

160   Wilson looked directly at Tom. He stood up on his toes and would have fallen to his knees if Tom hadn't supported him.

"Listen," said Tom, shaking him slightly. "I just arrived a minute ago from New York. I brought you the sports car we were discussing. The yellow car I was driving this afternoon wasn't mine."

The police officer sensed something in Tom's tone and looked over with a hostile glare.

"What's going on?" he demanded.

"I'm his friend," replied Tom, turning his head while still keeping his hands steady on Wilson's body. "He claims he knows the car that was involved... It was a yellow car."

The officer's suspicion prompted him to stare at Tom.

"And what color is your car?"

"It's a blue sports car."

Someone who had been driving a little behind us confirmed this, and the officer turned away.

"Now, if you can give me that correct name once more—"

Lifting Wilson like a toy, Tom carried him inside the office, placed him in a chair, and returned.

"If someone can come here and sit with him," he commanded. He observed as the two men closest to him exchanged reluctant glances and entered the room against their will. Then Tom closed the door behind them and descended the single step, avoiding eye contact with the table. As he walked near me, he whispered, "Let's leave."

161   With a sense of self-awareness, Tom confidently led the way through the growing crowd, nudging people aside. We passed a

hurried doctor, holding a case, who had been summoned with desperate hope only thirty minutes prior.

Tom drove at a slow pace until we were past the curve in the road. Then, he pressed down on the accelerator and the car sped through the night. After a while, I heard a quiet, raspy sob and noticed tears streaming down Tom's face.

"That coward!" he whimpered. "He didn't even stop his car."

THROUGH THE DARK, rustling trees, the Buchanan's house suddenly appeared. Tom parked the car next to the porch and looked up at the second floor, where two windows glowed among the vines.

"Daisy's home," he said. As we stepped out of the car, he glanced at me and slightly frowned.

"I should have dropped you off in West Egg, Nick. There's nothing we can do tonight."

A sense of determination enveloped him as he spoke seriously. As we walked across the moonlit gravel towards the porch, he summarized the situation in a few brisk sentences.

"I'll call a taxi to take you home, and while you wait, you and Jordan should go to the kitchen and have some supper if you're hungry." He opened the door. "Come inside."

"No, thank you. But I would appreciate it if you could arrange a taxi for me. I'll wait outside."

Jordan placed her hand on my arm.

"Why don't you come in, Nick?"

"No, thank you."

Feeling slightly ill, I desired some solitude. However, Jordan remained for a moment longer.

162   "It's not even nine-thirty yet," she said.

I refused to go inside; I had enough of everyone, including Jordan, for one day. She must have noticed my expression because she quickly turned away and ran up the porch steps into the house. I sat down for a few minutes, with my head in my hands, until I heard the phone being picked up inside and the butler calling for a taxi. Then I walked slowly down the driveway, away from the house, planning to wait by the gate.

I hadn't walked twenty yards when I heard my name, and Gatsby emerged from between two bushes onto the path. By that point, I must have been feeling pretty strange because all I could think about was the brightness of his pink suit under the moonlight.

"What are you doing?" I asked.

"Just standing here, old buddy."

For some reason, that seemed like a shameful thing to do. I couldn't help but wonder if he was planning to rob the house any minute now. I wouldn't have been surprised to see intimidating figures, perhaps "Wolfshiem's people," lurking in the dark bushes behind him.

"Did you see any trouble on the road?" he asked after a moment.

"Yes."

He hesitated.

"Was she killed?"

"Yes."

"I thought so; I told Daisy I thought so. It's better for the shock to hit all at once. She handled it pretty well."

He spoke as if Daisy's reaction was the only thing that mattered.

"I took a back road to get to West Egg," he continued, "and parked the car in my garage. I don't think anyone saw us, but I can't be certain."

I didn't like him so much by this time that I didn't think it was necessary to tell him he was wrong.

"Who was the woman?" he asked.

"Her name was Wilson. Her husband owns the garage. How did it happen?"

"Well, I tried to turn the wheel--" He stopped talking, and suddenly I guessed what had happened.

"Was Daisy driving?"

"Yes," he said after a moment, "but of course I'll say I was. You see, when we left New York she was very nervous and she thought it would calm her down to drive—and this woman came rushing out at us just as we were passing a car coming from the opposite direction. It all happened very quickly, but it felt to me like the woman wanted to speak to us, as if she thought we were someone she knew. Well, at first Daisy turned her head away from the woman towards the other car, and then she got scared and turned back. The second my hand reached the wheel, I felt the impact—it must have killed her instantly."

"It tore her open—"

"Don't tell me, old buddy," he winced. "Anyway—Daisy stepped on the gas. I tried to make her stop, but she couldn't, so I pulled the emergency brake. Then she fell onto my lap and I kept driving.

"She'll be okay by tomorrow," he said after a while. "I'm just going to wait here and see if he tries to bother her about what happened earlier. She's locked herself in her room, and if he tries anything aggressive, she's going to turn the light off and on again."

"He won't harm her," I said. "He's not thinking about her."

"I don't trust him, old buddy."

"How long do you plan on waiting?" I asked.

"All night, if needed. At least until everyone goes to bed."

A new thought occurred to me. What if Tom found out that Daisy had been driving? He might see a connection and interpret it in any way he wanted. I glanced at the house; a few windows were lit downstairs, and there was a soft pink glow coming from Daisy's room on the ground floor.

"You stay here," I said. "I'll check if there's any sign of trouble."

I walked along the edge of the lawn, stepped carefully on the gravel, and quietly climbed the steps of the porch. The curtains in the living room were open, and it appeared to be empty. I continued onto the porch where we had dined that June night, three months earlier. There was a small rectangle of light, which I assumed was the window to the pantry. The blind was partially closed, but there was a small gap at the bottom.

Daisy and Tom were sitting across from each other at the kitchen table, with a dish of cold fried chicken between them, along with two bottles of ale. Tom was speaking passionately, leaning across the table and his hand covered hers. Every so often, Daisy would look up at him and nod in agreement.

They didn't seem happy, yet neither did they seem unhappy. There was an undeniable sense of natural closeness in the scene, and anyone would think they were plotting together.

As I quietly stepped off the porch, I could hear the faint sound of my taxi approaching along the dark road towards the house. Gatsby was still waiting for me in the driveway, exactly where I had left him.

"Is everything calm up there?" he asked anxiously.

"Yes, it's all calm," I hesitated for a moment, considering my words. "You should come back home and get some rest."

He shook his head in disagreement.

"I want to stay here until Daisy goes to bed. Good night, my friend."

He slipped his hands into his coat pockets and turned back to the house. I walked away and left him there under the moonlight, standing watch over nothingness.

EIGHT

166   I COULDN'T SLEEP at all last night. At sunrise, I heard a taxi driving up Gatsby's driveway. I immediately got out of bed and started getting dressed. I felt like I had to warn him about something.

"Nothing happened," he said weakly. "I waited, and around four o'clock she came to the window, stood there for a minute, and then turned off the light."

That night, his house seemed bigger than ever to me as we searched the large rooms for cigarettes. It wasn't clean and full as it had been. We opened the French windows in the drawing-room and sat there smoking, looking out into the darkness.

"You should leave," I said. "It's pretty likely that they'll find your car."

"Leave now, my friend?"

"Go to Atlantic City for a week, or maybe up to Montreal."

167   He refused to think about it. Leaving Daisy behind was not even a possibility for him until he found out her plans. He was desperately holding onto a glimmer of hope, and I didn't have the heart to make him let go.

That night, he shared with me the peculiar tale of his past with

Dan Cody. He told me this story because the facade of "Jay Gatsby" had shattered under Tom's cruel words, and the elaborate charade was finally over. I believe he would have confessed anything at that moment, without holding back, but all he wanted to discuss was Daisy.

168   She was the first "nice" girl he had ever known. He had met people like her before, but there was always an invisible barrier between them. He found her incredibly attractive. At first, he and other officers from Camp Taylor visited her house. Then, he started going alone. He was amazed - he had never been in such a beautiful house before. But what made it even more special was that Daisy lived there. To her, it was as ordinary as his tent at camp was to him. The house had an aura of excitement, with hints of even more stunning and cool bedrooms upstairs, vibrant activities happening in its corridors, and love stories that were fresh and alive, not old and forgotten. It thrilled him to know that many men had loved Daisy before him, as it made her even more valuable in his eyes. He could feel their presence lingering in the house, filling the air with echoes of past emotions.

169   But he knew he was in Daisy's house by a huge accident. Although he had a promising future as Jay Gatsby, he was currently a young man with no money and no past. At any moment, his uniform might be taken away from him, leaving him with nothing. So, he made the most of his time. He took whatever he could get, greedily and without morals. Eventually, one October night, he took Daisy, realizing he had no right to touch her hand.

He could have despised himself because he had deceived Daisy. I don't mean that he lied about his wealth, but he had purposely made Daisy believe that he was similar to her, someone who could take care of her. In reality, he didn't have the same resources. He didn't have a supportive family and he was always at the mercy of the government, who could send him anywhere in the world.

However, he didn't despise himself and things didn't go as he expected. His original plan was probably to take what he could and move on, but now he found himself pursuing a goal like a knight searching for the Holy Grail. He knew Daisy was special, but he didn't realize how extraordinary a "nice" girl could be. She disappeared into her opulent house, with her luxurious and fulfilling life, leaving Gatsby with nothing. He felt tied to her, as if they were married, even though they weren't.

170   When they saw each other again, two days later, it was Gatsby who was out of breath and feeling somehow tricked. Daisy turned towards him and he kissed her. Gatsby felt overwhelmingly aware of the youth and mystery that money keeps locked away in wealthy women like Daisy.

❧

"I can't fully express how shocked I was to realize that I loved her, old sport. I even held onto a belief for a while that she might reject me, but she didn't, because she was in love with me too. She thought I was knowledgeable because I knew things that were different from what she knew. Well, there I was, far from achieving my ambitions, falling deeper in love every minute, and suddenly I didn't care. What was the point of accomplishing great things if I could have a better time sharing with her what I planned to do?"

171   On the afternoon right before he left for his trip abroad, he sat with Daisy in his arms for a long time without saying a word. It was a chilly autumn day, with a warm fire in the room and Daisy's cheeks flushed. Every now and then she would adjust herself, causing him to slightly readjust his arm, and at one point he kissed her dark, shiny hair. The afternoon brought them a sense of tranquility, as if wanting to give them a lasting memory to hold onto before their looming separation the next day. During their month of love, they had never been closer, nor communicated more deeply than in those moments when she gently brushed her silent lips against his shoulder or when he tenderly touched the tips of her fingers as if she were peacefully asleep.

~

HE PERFORMED EXCEPTIONALLY WELL in the war. He had already become a captain before he went to the front, and after the battles in Argonne, he achieved the rank of major and gained command of the divisional machine-guns. Following the armistice, he desperately tried to return home, but due to some complication or misunderstanding, he was instead sent to Oxford. Daisy's letters carried a sense of worry and a hint of despair. She couldn't understand why he couldn't come back. The weight of the outside world was pressuring her, and she longed to see him, to feel his presence by her side, and to be reassured that she was making the right decisions after all.

172 For Daisy was young and her fancy world was filled with beautiful flowers and pleasant, cheerful snobbery. During the quiet tea hour, there were always rooms filled with a constant, gentle excitement, while new faces floated around like delicate rose petals swaying to the sad music.

In this hazy world, Daisy began to resume her social activities with the change of the season. Suddenly, she was once again going on multiple dates each day with different men. Yet, deep inside, she felt a longing for a decision. She wanted her life to take shape quicklly and that was within reach.

That powerful influence came into her life during the middle of spring, when Tom Buchanan arrived. There was a strong, solid presence about him, both physically and in his social standing, and Daisy was flattered. There was surely some internal struggle and relief. The letter arrived for Gatsby while he was still at Oxford.

~

173 IT WAS early morning on Long Island and we went around opening the rest of the windows downstairs, letting in the soft, grayish-golden light. The shadow of a tree stretched across the dewy ground,

and faint birdsong filled the air amidst the blue leaves. There was a gentle, tranquil breeze, promising a cool and beautiful day ahead.

"I don't think she ever truly loved him." Gatsby turned away from the window and looked at me challengingly. "You have to understand, old friend, she was very emotional this afternoon. He said things to her in a way that frightened her, making it seem like I was some kind of dishonest person. As a result, she hardly knew what she was saying."

He sank into a chair with a sense of despair.

"Of course, she might have loved him for a brief moment when they first got married--and maybe even loved me more back then, do you see?"

Suddenly, he made an intriguing remark.

"Regardless," he said, "it was just personal."

What else could you gather from his statement, except to suspect that there was an intense meaning to the situation that couldn't be easily understood?

He returned from France when Tom and Daisy were still on their honeymoon and made a sad but irresistible trip to Louisville with the last of his army pay. He stayed there for a week, walking the streets where they had walked together at night and revisiting the places they had gone to in her white car. Just as Daisy's house had always seemed more mysterious and lively to him than other houses, his idea of the city itself, even without her, was filled with a melancholy beauty.

He left with a feeling that if he had searched harder, he might have found her--that he was leaving her behind. The day-coach he rode in now, as he was broke, was hot. He went out to the open vestibule and sat on a folding chair, watching the station slide away and unfamiliar buildings pass by. Then they moved out into the spring fields, and for a brief moment a yellow trolley raced alongside them, carrying people who might have seen the enchanting sight of her pale face on a casual street.

The track curved and now they were going away from the sun,

which, as it sank lower, seemed to spread a comforting glow over the disappearing city where she had breathed. He reached out his hand desperately, as if trying to snatch just a bit of the air, to save a fragment of the place that she had made beautiful for him. But everything was passing too quickly for his blurry eyes, and he knew that he had lost the freshest and finest part forever.

175   It was nine o'clock when we finished eating breakfast and went outside onto the porch. The night had caused a noticeable change in the weather, and there was a hint of autumn in the air. The gardener, the last of Gatsby's former servants, came to the bottom of the steps.

"I'm planning on draining the pool today, Mr. Gatsby. Leaves will start falling soon, and there's always trouble with the pipes."

"Don't do it today," Gatsby replied. He turned to me with an apologetic look. "You know, old buddy, I never even used that pool all summer?"

I checked the time on my watch and stood up.

"I have twelve minutes until my train."

I didn't want to go to the city. I wasn't good enough for any meaningful work, but it was more than that--I didn't want to leave Gatsby. I missed that train, and then another, before I could bring myself to leave.

"I'll give you a call," I finally said.

"Please do, old buddy."

"I'll call you around noon."

We walked down the steps slowly.

"I guess Daisy will call too." He looked at me anxiously, as if he hoped I would confirm this.

"I suppose so."

"Well, goodbye."

We shook hands and I started to leave. Just before I reached the hedge, I remembered something and turned around.

"They're a terrible group of people," I shouted across the lawn. "You're worth more than all of them combined."

176   I'm glad I spoke up then. It was the only nice thing I ever said to

him, because I didn't approve of him at all. At first, he nodded politely, and then he smiled with understanding, as if we had been in complete agreement about that all along. His flashy pink suit stood out against the white steps, and it reminded me of the night when I first came to his old family home, three months earlier. The lawn and driveway had been filled with people who suspected him of being corrupt, and he stood on those steps, hiding his uncorrupted dream, waving goodbye to them.

I thanked him for his hospitality. We were always thanking him for that--me and the others.

"Goodbye," I called. "I enjoyed breakfast, Gatsby."

BACK IN THE CITY, I tried to make a list of the stock quotes for a while, but then I dozed off in my swivel chair. Just before noon, the phone woke me up, and I jolted awake with sweat on my forehead. It was Jordan Baker; she often called me around this time because she was hard to reach due to her constant moving between hotels, clubs, and private houses. Normally, her voice sounded fresh and cool, as if a divot from a golf course had flown in through the office window, but this morning it seemed harsh and dry.

"I left Daisy's house," she said over the phone. "I'm in Hempstead right now, and later today I'm heading to Southampton."

It was probably the right move to leave Daisy's house, but I was annoyed by her actions, and her next comment only aggravated me more.

"You weren't very nice to me last night."

"How could that have mattered at the time?"

There was a moment of silence. Then she spoke up again.

"Either way, I want to see you."

"I want to see you too."

"What if I don't go to Southampton and come into town this afternoon?"

"No, I don't think this afternoon will work."

"Alright then."

"It's impossible this afternoon. Various--"

We continued talking like that for a while, but then our conversation abruptly ended. I'm not sure which one of us hung up with a sharp sound, but I didn't care. I couldn't have spoken to her across a tea table that day, even if I never spoke to her again in this world.

A few minutes later, I tried calling Gatsby's house, but the line was busy. I made four attempts, and finally an impatient operator informed me that the line was being kept open for a long-distance call from Detroit. I marked the 3:50 train on my timetable with a small circle. Then, I leaned back in my chair and tried to think. It was only noon.

178 As I rode the train that morning in silence. I moved away from others to avoid hearing them talking about Myrtle. Myrtle Wilson's tragic death would eventually be forgotten. Now, I want to backtrack a bit and explain what occurred at the garage after we left there the night before.

They had trouble finding Myrtle's sister, Catherine. It seemed that she had broken her own rule against drinking that night because when she finally arrived, she was drunk and couldn't comprehend that the ambulance had already headed to Flushing. When they managed to convince her of this fact, she immediately fainted as if that was the most unbearable part of the whole situation. Someone, whether out of kindness or curiosity, offered to drive her in their car and follow the ambulance carrying her sister's body.

179 Late into the night, a gathering crowd pressed against the front of the garage, as George Wilson anxiously rocked back and forth on the couch inside. For a time, the office door remained open, tempting everyone who entered the garage to glance through it. Eventually, someone expressed their dismay and closed the door. Michaelis and a few other men were present; at first, there were four or five men, then later only two or three. Eventually, Michaelis had to request that the last stranger wait an additional fifteen minutes, allowing

him to return to his own place and brew some coffee. After that, he remained alone with Wilson until dawn.

Around three o'clock, Wilson's incoherent mutterings took on a new tone—he grew quieter and began discussing the yellow car. He proclaimed that he had a method for discovering the owner of the yellow car and then blurted out that a couple of months ago, his wife had returned from the city with a bruised face and swollen nose.

But as soon as he heard himself utter these words, he recoiled and started crying out "Oh, my God!" once again, with a strained voice. Michaelis made a clumsy attempt to divert his attention.

"How long have you been married, George? Come on, try to sit still for a moment and answer my question. How long have you been married?"

"Twelve years."

"Have you ever had any children? Come on, George, sit still—I asked you a question. Have you ever had any children?"

The dark brown beetles kept banging against the dim light, and whenever Michaelis heard a car racing along the road outside, it sounded like the car that hadn't stopped a few hours earlier. He didn't want to enter the garage because the workbench was stained from where the body had been lying. So, he uncomfortably walked around the office, knowing every object in it by morning, and occasionally sat beside Wilson, trying to keep him calmer.

"Do you have a church that you sometimes go to, George? Even if it's been a while? Maybe I could contact the church and have a priest come over to talk to you, you know?"

"I don't belong to any."

"You should have a church, George, especially in times like these. You must have gone to church at some point. Didn't you get married in a church? Listen, George, listen to me. Didn't you get married in a church?"

"That was a long time ago."

His effort to respond disrupted the rhythm of his rocking, and he fell silent for a moment. Then, the same partly knowing, partly confused expression returned to his faded eyes.

"Look in that drawer over there," he said, pointing at the desk.

"Which drawer?"

"That drawer--that one."

Michaelis opened the drawer closest to his hand. There was nothing in it except a small, expensive dog leash, made of leather and braided silver. It appeared to be brand new.

"This?" he asked, holding it up.

Wilson stared and nodded.

"I found it yesterday. My wife tried to tell me about it, but I knew it was something strange."

"You mean your wife bought it?"

"She had it wrapped on her dresser."

Michaelis didn't see anything odd about that, and he gave Wilson a dozen reasons why his wife might have bought the dog leash. But it's possible that Wilson had heard similar explanations before from Myrtle because he started whispering "Oh, my God!" again, leaving several explanations up in the air.

"Then he killed her," said Wilson. Suddenly, his mouth dropped open.

"Who did?"

"I have a way of finding out."

"You're being pessimistic, George," said his friend. "This has been hard on you, and you don't know what you're saying. You should try to sit quietly until morning."

"He murdered her."

"It was an accident, George."

Wilson shook his head. His eyes became narrower and his mouth slightly wider with a hint of superiority.

"I know," he said confidently. "I'm one of those trusting guys, and I don't suspect anyone of any harm, but when I know something, I know it. It was the man in that car. She ran out to talk to him, and he wouldn't stop."

Michaelis had noticed this too, but he hadn't thought there was anything particularly important about it. He believed that Mrs. Wilson was running away from her husband, rather than trying to stop a specific car.

"How could she be like that?"

"She's mysterious," said Wilson, as if that answered the question. "Ah-h-h—"

182 He started rocking again, and Michaelis stood there twisting the leash in his hand.

"Do you have a friend I could call for you, George?"

Michaelis knew it was a hopeless request. He was almost certain that Wilson had no friends; he wasn't enough for his wife. However, he felt a slight relief when he noticed a change in the room, a blue light appearing by the window. He realized that dawn was approaching. Around five o'clock, it was bright enough outside to turn off the light.

Wilson's glazed eyes gazed out at the ash-heaps, where small grey clouds moved in strange patterns in the gentle morning breeze.

"I talked to her," he muttered, breaking the long silence. "I told her she may deceive me, but she can't deceive God. I brought her to the window"—he made an effort to get up and walked to the back window, pressing his face against it—"and I said, 'God knows every little thing you've been doing. You may trick me, but you can't trick God!'"

Standing behind him, Michaelis was shocked to see that Wilson was staring at the eyes of Doctor T. J. Eckleburg that had just emerged, pale and enormous, from the disappearing darkness.

"God sees everything," Wilson repeated.

"That's an advertisement," Michaelis told him.

183 BY SIX O'CLOCK, Michaelis was tired and grateful when he heard a car stop outside. It was one of the people who had been watching

Wilson the night before. They had promised to come back, so Michaelis cooked breakfast for the three of them and they ate together. Wilson was quieter now, and Michaelis went home to sleep. Four hours later, when he rushed back to the garage, Wilson was gone.

People later found out that Wilson had been walking the whole time. They were able to trace his movements. First, he went to Port Roosevelt and then to Gad's Hill. At Gad's Hill, he bought a sandwich that he didn't eat and a cup of coffee. It seems like he was tired because he was walking slowly. He didn't reach Gad's Hill until noon. So far, it wasn't hard to figure out what he was doing. Some boys saw him acting strangely, and drivers saw him staring at them oddly from the side of the road. After that, he disappeared for three hours. Based on what he said to Michaelis, the police believed that he spent that time going from garage to garage in the area, asking about a yellow car. But no garage owner ever came forward to say they saw him. Maybe he had an easier way of finding the information he wanted. By two-thirty, he was in West Egg. He asked someone for directions to Gatsby's house. So, by that time, he already knew Gatsby's name.

184   At two o'clock, Gatsby changed into his swimming suit and told the butler to let him know if anyone called while he was at the pool. He stopped by the garage to get a pool float. He reminded the butler that the car should not be taken out.

Carrying the mattress on his shoulder, Gatsby made his way to the pool.

No phone message arrived, but the dedicated butler stayed awake, waiting for it until four o'clock. Gatsby was entering a new world, one that seemed real but lacked substance, where lost souls, breathing dreams like air, drifted aimlessly. Meanwhile, a strange figure was moving toward him behind the trees.

185   The driver, who was mentored by Wolfshiem, heard the gunshots but didn't think much of them. I immediately rushed to Gatsby's house from the train station. When I got to the house,

without speaking a word, the chauffeur, butler, gardener, and I hurried to the pool.

There was a slight, barely noticeable movement of the water as the fresh current from one end pushed towards the drain at the other. The float moved unevenly down the pool, its unintended cargo floating on top. It traced a thin red circle in the pool.

It wasn't until we started towards the house with Gatsby's bodu that the gardener saw Wilson's body a short distance away in the grass, and the tragedy was complete.

CHAPTER
NINE

186   AFTER TWO YEARS, I can only recall bits and pieces of that day, the night that followed, and the next day. It all blends together in my memory as a constant stream of police officers, photographers, and journalists going in and out of Gatsby's front door. A rope was placed across the main gate, and a policeman stood guard to keep out the curious onlookers. However, a few clever boys soon discovered they could sneak into the yard through mine, and they would gather around the pool, their mouths agape with wonder. I overheard someone, who appeared to be a confident figure, possibly a detective, labeling Wilson's lifeless body as that of a "madman" that afternoon. The authoritative tone in his voice set the tone for the newspaper reports the following morning.

187   Most of those reports were like a nightmare. They were over-the-top and some were inaccurate. When Michaelis testified, he brought to light Wilson's suspicions about his wife. I thought for sure that this scandalous story would be turned into a larger one. But Myrtle's sister, Catherine, declared that her sister had never met Gatsby. She insisted that her sister was perfectly content with her husband and had stayed out of trouble. Catherine convinced herself of this. She

could not let her sister's death be attached to the idea of her own wrongdoing. So, to simplify matters, Wilson was portrayed as a grief-stricken man who had lost his sanity. This allowed the case to be dealt with more easily, and then it was put to rest.

However, all these details seemed distant and irrelevant. I found myself sympathizing with Gatsby and feeling alone. As word of the tragedy spread to the village of West Egg, I became the go-to person for any information or practical questions about Gatsby. Initially, I was taken aback and confused by this responsibility, but as Gatsby lay unmoving and silent in his house for hours on end, it became clear to me that I was the only one who cared--cared with the sort of personal investment that, in some vague way, I felt was owed to him in the end.

188   I called Daisy thirty minutes after we found him, calling her without hesitation. But she and Tom had left early that afternoon, taking their things with them.

"Did they leave an address?"

"No."

"Did they say when they would return?"

"No."

"Do you have any idea where they are or how I can reach them?"

"I don't know. Can't say."

I wanted to find someone for him. I wanted to go into the room where he lay and reassure him: "I'll find someone for you, Gatsby. Don't worry. Just trust me and I'll find someone for you."

Meyer Wolfshiem's name was not in the phone book. The butler gave me his office address on Broadway, and I called Information, but by the time I got the number it was already past five, and no one answered the phone.

"Can you try calling again?"

"I've already called three times."

"It's very important."

"Sorry, I'm afraid no one is there."

I returned to the drawing room and for a moment I thought that the people who suddenly filled it were chance visitors. But even as they pulled back the sheet and looked at Gatsby with shocked eyes, his plea echoed in my mind:

"Listen, my friend, you must find someone for me. You have to try your best. I can't go through this alone."

I broke away from someone who started asking me questions and quickly went upstairs to search through the unlocked parts of Gatsby's desk. He had never confirmed whether his parents were alive or dead. However, I found nothing except for a picture of Dan Cody, a reminder of forgotten violence, staring down from the wall.

The next morning, I sent the butler to New York with a letter to Wolfshiem. In the letter, I asked for information and urged him to come out on the next train. At the time, the request seemed unnecessary. I was certain that he would startle when he saw the newspapers, just as I was certain that I would receive a wire from Daisy before noon. However, neither a wire nor Mr. Wolfshiem arrived. The only ones who did arrive were more police officers, photographers, and newspaper reporters. When the butler returned with Wolfshiem's response, a sense of defiance and scornful unity between Gatsby and myself against all of them began to surface.

Dear Mr. Carraway,

This news has been one of the most shocking events in my life. I can barely believe that it is true. The man's reckless actions should make us all reflect. I am unable to come down at the moment, as I am currently engaged in some incredibly important business and cannot involve myself in this matter right now. If there is anything I can do at a later time, please inform me through a letter addressed to Edgar. When I hear about such a thing, I am completely astounded and devastated.

Sincerely,

Meyer Wolfshiem

P.S. Please inform me about the funeral arrangements, as I am not acquainted with his family.

When the phone rang that afternoon and Long Distance said

Chicago was calling, I thought it would finally be Daisy on the line. However, it was a man's voice, weak and distant.

"This is Slagle speaking…"

"Yes?" I didn't recognize the name.

"Terrible situation, isn't it? Did you receive my message?"

"I haven't received any messages."

"Young Parke is in trouble," he hurriedly explained. "They caught him handing over the bonds at the counter. Just five minutes before, they received a notice from New York with the bond numbers. Can you believe it? These small towns are unpredictable…"

"Hello!" I interrupted, out of breath. "Listen here—this isn't Mr. Gatsby. Mr. Gatsby has passed away."

There was a long silence on the other end of the line, followed by an exclamation… and then a sudden disconnect.

I BELIEVE it was on the third day when a telegram arrived, signed by Henry C. Gatz, from a town in Minnesota. It simply stated that the sender was leaving immediately and requested that the funeral be postponed until his arrival.

Gatsby's father arrived, an elderly man who appeared solemn, helpless, and distressed. He was bundled up in a long, inexpensive coat despite the warm day in September. His eyes continuously leaked with excitement, and I took hold of his bag and umbrella as he pulled anxiously at his thin, gray beard. It was a struggle to remove his coat, as he was on the verge of collapsing. I guided him into the music room and insisted he sit down while I arranged for some food. However, he refused to eat and accidentally spilled the glass of milk due to his trembling hand.

He said, "I read about it in the newspaper from Chicago. The whole story was there. I came right away."

"I didn't know how to get in touch with you."

His eyes, unfocused, wandered restlessly around the room.

"He must have been insane," he muttered. "That man must have been insane."

"Would you like some coffee?" I suggested.

"No, I don't want anything. I'm okay now, Mr.--"

"Carraway."

"Well, I'm fine now. Where is Jimmy?"

I escorted him into the living room, where his son was lying, and left him there. A few young boys had gathered on the steps, peeking into the hallway. When I informed them about the visitor's identity, they left reluctantly.

After a short while, Mr. Gatz opened the door and came out. His mouth was slightly open, his face a bit flushed, and tears were streaming from his eyes. He had reached an age where death was no longer a shocking surprise. As he looked around and took in the grandeur of the hall and the rooms opening up from it, his sorrow started to mix with a sense of proud awe. I guided him to an upstairs bedroom. While he removed his coat and vest, I informed him that all the arrangements had been postponed until his arrival.

"I didn't know what you would want, Mr. Gatsby—"

"Gatz is my name."

"—Mr. Gatz. I thought you might want to take the body out West."

He shook his head.

"Jimmy always preferred the East. He established himself there. Were you a friend of my son's, Mr.—?"

"We were very close friends."

"He had a bright future ahead of him, you know. He was still young, but he possessed a great deal of intelligence."

He gestured towards his head, emphasizing his point, and I nodded.

"If he had lived, he would have become a remarkable man. A man like James J. Hill. He would have played a role in the development of our country."

"That is true," I responded, feeling uncomfortable.

He fumbled with the embroidered coverlet, attempting to remove it from the bed, and then lay down rigidly—quickly falling asleep.

Later that night, a clearly anxious person called, insisting on knowing my identity before sharing his name.

"This is Mr. Carraway," I stated.

"Oh!" He sounded relieved. "This is Klipspringer."

I was relieved too because it seemed like another friend would be at Gatsby's funeral. I didn't want it to be in the newspapers and attract a crowd of tourists, so I had been calling a few people myself. It was difficult to find them.

"The funeral is tomorrow," I said. "At three o'clock, here at the house. I hope you can let anyone who might be interested know."

"Oh, I will," he said hurriedly. "Although I probably won't see anyone, but if I do."

His tone made me suspicious.

"Of course, you'll be there too."

"Well, I'll try my best. Actually, the truth is that I'm staying with some people in Greenwich, and they expect me to be with them tomorrow. They have planned a sort of picnic or something. But I'll do everything I can to get away."

I exclaimed, "Huh!" without holding back, and he must have heard me because he continued nervously:

"The reason I called was because I left a pair of shoes there. I wonder if it would be too much trouble to have the butler send them to me. You see, they are tennis shoes, and I'm somewhat helpless without them. My address is care of B. F.—"

I didn't hear the rest of the name because I hung up the phone.

After that, I felt a bit ashamed for Gatsby.

On the morning of the funeral, I decided to go to New York to speak with Meyer Wolfshiem. I couldn't reach him any other way. When I got to his office, a beautiful Jewish woman opened an interior door and stared at me with unfriendly eyes.

"No one's here," she stated. "Mr. Wolfshiem has gone to Chicago."

Just then, I clearly heard Wolfshiem's voice calling for "Stella!" from the other side of the door.

"Leave your name on the desk," she quickly instructed. "I'll give it to him when he returns."

"But I know he's there."

She took a step towards me and angrily placed her hands on her hips.

"You boys think you can just barge in here whenever you want," she scolded. "We're getting tired of it. When I say he's in Chicago, he's in Chicago."

I mentioned Gatsby.

"Oh-h!" She looked at me again. "Can you at least tell me your name?"

She disappeared. In a moment, Meyer Wolfshiem stood in the doorway, extending both hands solemnly. He brought me into his office, speaking in a respectful tone about how it was a sad time for all of us, and offering me a cigar.

"I remember the first time I met him," he said. "He was a young officer fresh out of the army, covered in medals he earned during the war. He was so poor that he had to keep wearing his uniform because he couldn't afford regular clothes. The first time I saw him was when he walked into Winebrenner's poolroom on Forty-third Street and asked for a job. He hadn't eaten anything for a couple of days. 'Come on, have lunch with me,' I said. He ate more than four dollars' worth of food in just thirty minutes."

"Did you help him start his business?" I asked.

"Help him? I made him," he responded.

"I raised him up from nothing, straight out of the streets. I imme-diately recognized that he was a well-mannered and respectable young man, and when he told me he went to Oggsford, I knew I could put him to good use. I convinced him to join the American Legion, and he quickly gained a good reputation there. Right away, he did some work for one of my clients in Albany. We were insepa-rable in everything"—he held up two large fingers—"always together."

I wondered if this partnership had included the World Series transaction in 1919.

"He's dead now," I said after a moment. "You were his closest friend. Come to his funeral this afternoon."

He seemed emotional, as tears welled up in his eyes when he shook his head and said, "I can't do it—I can't get involved."

"There's nothing to get involved in. It's all over now."

"When a man gets killed, I never like to get involved in any way. I prefer to stay out of it. When I was younger, it was different. If a friend of mine died, no matter how, I stayed with them till the very end. You might think that's sentimental, but I mean it—to the bitter end."

Realizing that he was determined not to come for his own reasons, I stood up.

"Are you a college man?" he suddenly asked.

For a moment, I thought he was going to suggest something complex, but he only nodded and shook my hand.

"Let's learn to show our friendship for a man when he's alive and not after he's dead," he suggested. "After that, my own rule is to let everything be."

When I left his office, the sky had turned dark, and I returned to West Egg in a light rain. After changing my clothes, I went next door and found Mr. Gatz walking excitedly in the hallway. His pride in his son and his son's possessions continued to grow, and now he had something to show me.

"Jimmy sent me this picture," he said nervously, taking out his wallet. "Look at it."

It was a photograph of the house, worn and dirty with finger-prints on the corners. He eagerly pointed out every detail to me. "Look here!" he said, seeking approval in my eyes. He had shown it so many times that it seemed more real to him than the actual house.

"Jimmy sent it to me. I think it's a nice picture. It shows up well."

"Very nice. Have you seen him recently?"

"He came to visit me two years ago and bought me the house I live in now. We were upset when he ran away from home, but now I understand why he did it. He knew he had a bright future ahead of him. And ever since he became successful, he has been very generous to me."

Reluctantly, he put away the picture, holding it in front of my eyes for another moment. Then he returned the wallet and took out a worn-out book called Hopalong Cassidy from his pocket.

"Look here, this is a book he had when he was a boy. It just goes to show."

He opened it to the back cover and turned it around for me to see. On the last page, the word "schedule" was printed, followed by the date September 12, 1906. And underneath it:

Wake up - 6:00 am

Exercise and stretching - 6:15–6:30

Study electricity, etc. - 7:15–8:15

Work - 8:30–4:30

Baseball and sports - 4:30–5:00

Practice public speaking, poise, and how to improve - 5:00–6:00

Study necessary inventions - 7:00–9:00

General Resolutions

No more wasting time at Shafters or [a name, indecipherable]. No more smoking or chewing. Take a bath every other day. Read one educational book or magazine per week. Save $3.00 per week. Be more respectful to parents.

"I stumbled upon this book by chance," said the elderly man. "It just goes to show, doesn't it?"

"It certainly does."

"Jimmy was determined to succeed. He always had resolutions like these. Do you see what he wrote about improving his mind? He was always enthusiastic about that. He once told me I ate like a pig, and I got angry with him for it."

He hesitated to close the book, reading each item aloud and then eagerly looking at me. I think he expected me to write down the list for myself.

A little before three, the Lutheran minister from Flushing arrived, and I started to anxiously look out the windows for other cars. Gatsby's father did the same. As time passed and the servants gathered and waited in the hallway, his eyes blinked nervously, and he spoke about the rain in a worried, uncertain manner. The minister checked his watch multiple times, so I pulled him aside and asked if he could wait for another half an hour. But it was pointless. Nobody came.

199   AROUND FIVE O'CLOCK, we arrived at the cemetery in a procession of three cars. It was drizzling heavily, and we parked next to the gate. First, there was a gloomy black hearse, followed by Mr. Gatz, the minister, and me in the limousine. A little later, a few servants and the postman from West Egg arrived in Gatsby's station wagon, all completely soaked. As we entered the cemetery, I heard a car stop, followed by the sound of someone splashing through the wet ground behind us. I turned around and saw the man with glasses shaped like owl eyes. I had met him once before in the library, where he had been amazed by Gatsby's books.

I hadn't seen him since then, and I didn't know how he found out about the funeral or even his name. The rain poured down on his glasses, and he had to take them off to wipe them clean so he could see the protective covering over Gatsby's grave. For a moment, I tried to think about Gatsby, but he felt distant, and all I could remember was that Daisy hadn't sent any message or flowers. Dimly, I heard someone say, "Blessed are the dead that the rain falls on," and the man with owl eyes bravely replied, "Amen to that."

We hurriedly made our way back to the cars, soaking wet from the rain. By the gate, the man with owl eyes spoke to me.

"I couldn't get to the house," he commented.

"Nobody could," I replied.

"Unbelievable!" He exclaimed. "They used to come there in large numbers."

He took off his glasses and wiped them clean once more, both on the outside and inside.

200   "The poor man," he said.

ONE OF MY strongest memories is of returning home to the West after finishing school and later college, during the Christmas season. At six o'clock on a December evening, those who traveled beyond Chicago would gather at the old Union Station. I recall the girls returning from fancy boarding schools, wearing fur coats, and the sound of their breath freezing and causing them to chatter. We would wave our hands overhead when we spotted familiar faces and quickly exchange invitations.

As we pulled away into the winter night, encountering the real snow and watching it sparkle against the windows, the dim lights from small Wisconsin train stations passed by. Suddenly, there was a sharp, exhilarating chill in the air. We took deep breaths.

201   That's the Midwest I know. I don't think of the fields of wheat or the vast prairies. I am proud of growing up in the Carraway house in a city where houses are still known by a family's name throughout the years. Now I see that this has been a story about the Midwest, after all. Tom and Gatsby, Daisy and Jordan, and I, we were all from the Midwest, and perhaps we all shared some common flaw that made us somewhat unfit for life on the East Coast.

202   Even when I was most captivated by the East, when I was acutely aware of its superiority. West Egg, in particular, often appeared in my wildest dreams. In my mind, it resembled a night scene in a painting. However, the painting was dark and sad, with people ignoring each other.

After Gatsby's death, the East haunted me in that same manner. I made the decision to return home.

Before I departed, there was one task that needed to be completed, an uncomfortable and unpleasant task that may have been wiser to avoid. Yet, I wanted to leave things in order, not merely relying on the accommodating and indifferent sea to carry away my discarded belongings. I met with Jordan Baker and discussed what had transpired between us and what had occurred in my life afterwards. She sat perfectly still, listening attentively, in a large armchair.

She was dressed in golf attire, and I thought she looked like a great illustration, her chin held slightly high, her hair the color of an autumn leaf, and her face the same warm brown shade as the fingerless glove on her knee. When I finished speaking, she told me, without any reaction, that she was engaged to another man. I doubted this, even though there were a few men she could have easily married. However, I pretended to be surprised. For a brief moment, I questioned if I was making a mistake, but then I quickly reviewed everything in my mind and stood up to bid her farewell.

"Nevertheless, you did reject me," Jordan unexpectedly interjected. "You rejected me over the phone. I don't care about you now, but it was a new experience for me, and I felt a little disoriented for a while."

We shook hands.

"Oh, and do you remember," she added, "a conversation we had once about driving a car?"

"Well, not exactly," I replied.

"You said that a bad driver is only safe until they encounter another bad driver, right? Well, I encountered another bad driver, didn't I? I mean, it was foolish of me to make such a mistaken assumption. I thought you were someone who was honest and straightforward. I thought it was something you took pride in."

"I'm thirty," I confessed. "I'm five years too old to deceive myself and pretend it's honorable."

She didn't respond. Angry, partly in love with her, and incredibly sorry, I turned away.

~

204   ONE AFTERNOON IN LATE OCTOBER, I saw Tom Buchanan. He was walking ahead of me on Fifth Avenue, moving with a sense of alertness and aggression. His hands were slightly extended from his body, as if he was ready to defend himself from any interference. His head moved swiftly, scanning the surroundings with restless eyes. As I slowed down to avoid passing him, he suddenly stopped and focused his gaze on the display windows of a jewelry store. In that moment, he noticed my presence and walked back towards me, extending his hand for a handshake.

"What's the matter, Nick? Do you have a problem with shaking my hand?"

"Yes. You know very well what I think of you."

"You're insane, Nick," he quickly replied. "Insane as hell. I have no idea what's wrong with you."

"Tom," I asked, "what did you say to Wilson that afternoon?"

He stared at me in silence, confirming my correct assumption about those missing hours. I began to turn away, but he swiftly stepped forward and grabbed my arm.

"I told him the truth," he admitted. "He arrived at the door while we were preparing to leave, and when I sent word down to him that we were not at home, he tried to force his way upstairs. He was crazy enough to harm me if I hadn't revealed who owned the car. His hand hovered over a concealed revolver in his pocket the entire time he was in the house—" He stopped defiantly. "So what if I did tell him? That man deserved it. He deceived you just as he did Daisy, but he was a tough character. He ran over Myrtle as if she were a dog and didn't even bother to stop his car."

205   There was nothing I could say, except the one thing that I couldn't say out loud.

"And if you think I didn't have my share of suffering—look here, when I went to give up that apartment and saw that dang box of dog treats sitting there on the table, I sat down and cried like a baby. It was terrible—"

I couldn't forgive him or like him, but I saw that what he had done made sense to him. It was all very careless and confusing. They were careless people, Tom and Daisy—they destroyed things and living beings and then retreated back into their wealth or their lack of concern, or whatever it was that kept them together, and let others clean up the mess they'd made...

I shook hands with him; it seemed silly not to, because suddenly I felt like I was talking to a child. Then he went into the jewelry store to buy a pearl necklace—or maybe just a pair of cufflinks—free from my small-town uneasiness forever.

GATSBY'S HOUSE was still empty when I left—the grass on his lawn had grown as long as mine. One of the taxi drivers in the town never went past the entrance gate without stopping for a minute and pointing inside; maybe it was him who drove Daisy and Gatsby over to East Egg the night of the accident, and maybe he had created his own story about it. I didn't want to hear it and I avoided him when I got off the train.

I used to spend my Saturday nights in New York because his extravagant, dazzling parties stayed with me so vividly that I could still hear the music and laughter, faint but constant, coming from his garden, and the cars coming and going on his driveway. One night, I did hear a real car there, and I saw its headlights stop at his front steps. But I didn't investigate. It was probably some last-minute guest who had been away and didn't know that the party was over.

On the final night, with my suitcase packed and my car sold to the local store, I went over and looked at that enormous, chaoti, failure of a house one more time. On the bright steps, an inappropriate word, scribbled by a young boy with a piece of brick, stood out clearly in the moonlight. I erased it, scraping my shoe roughly against the stone. Then, I wandered down to the beach and stretched out on the sand.

207   Most of the popular beach destinations were closed at this time and there were only a few lights visible.

While sitting there, reflecting on this ancient and unfamiliar world, I thought about Gatsby's amazement when he first saw the green light at the end of Daisy's dock. He had traveled a long way to reach this grand estate, and his dreams must have felt within reach. Little did he know that his dreams were already in the past. They were in the vast darkness beyond the city, where the unknown fields of the country stretched out beneath the night sky.

Gatsby had faith in the green light, a symbol of an exciting future that seems to get further away with each passing year. Though we couldn't grasp it back then, it doesn't matter. It's true that tomorrow we will work even harder, reaching out further with our hopes and dreams. And one beautiful morning—

208   And so we continue, our boats pushing against the current, constantly pulled back into the past.